I'M KNEELING NEXT to Katherine's body, my heart racing, my breaths shallow and fast, my emotions reeling crazily at the sight on the ground before me. Katherine is lying on her side, curled up, as if she was cowering from whoever attacked her. Her body is still warm, but there's no pulse. And that means she's dead. *Dead!* It can't be possible. Katherine . . . who I've gone to school with, been friends—and enemies—with. I can't believe that this is happening.

THE TODD STRASSER "THRILL"-OGY

Wish You Were Dead
Blood on My Hands
Kill You Last

* * *

OTHER EGMONT USA BOOKS YOU MAY ENJOY

Candor
by Pam Bachorz

Epitaph Road
by David Patneaude

family
by Micol Ostow

The Tension of Opposites
by Kristina McBride

blood on my hands

TODD STRASSER

EGMONT
USA
NEW YORK

EGMONT

We bring stories to life

First published by Egmont USA, 2010
This paperback edition published by Egmont USA, 2011
443 Park Avenue South, Suite 806
New York, NY 10016

1 3 5 7 9 8 6 4 2

www.egmontusa.com
www.toddstrasser.com

THE LIBRARY OF CONGRESS HAS CATALOGED THE HARDCOVER EDITION AS FOLLOWS:

Strasser, Todd.
Blood on my hands / Todd Strasser.
p. cm.
Summary: At a high school party, a girl finds her best friend murdered, only to be discovered
holding the weapon and accused of the crime.
ISBN 978-1-60684-023-8 (hardcover) — 978-1-60684-239-3 (eBook)
[1. Murder—Fiction. 2. Love—Fiction. 3. Mystery and detective stories.] I. Title.
PZ7.S899Bl 2010
[Fic]—dc22
2010023901

Paperback ISBN 978-1-60684-228-7

Printed in the United States of America

CPSIA tracking label information:
Printed in July 2011 at Berryville Graphics, Berryville, Virginia

To Lisa Dolan,
who lives and breathes literacy

I would like to thank the following people for their
contributions toward bringing this story to life:
Regina Griffin, Greg Ferguson,
Dr. Petra Deistler-Kaufmann, Tina Pantginis,
and Augusta Klein.

"You know that when I hate you, it is because I love you to a point of passion that unhinges my soul."
— JULIE-JEANNE-ÉLÉANORE DE LESPINASSE,
    French salonist (1732–1776)

"Keep your friends close, and your enemies closer."
— SUN-TZU, Chinese general and military strategist
    (~400 BC)

blood
on
my
hands

chapter 1

Saturday 11:45 P.M.

IN THE DARK woods behind the baseball dugout, I'm kneeling next to Katherine's body, my heart racing, my breaths shallow and fast, my emotions reeling crazily at the sight on the ground before me. Katherine is lying on her side, curled up, as if she was cowering from whoever attacked her. Her body is still warm, but there's no pulse. I know because I just pressed my index and middle fingers against her sticky wet neck and then to her wrist to feel her carotid and radial arteries, the ones the EMTs told me they checked. And that means she's dead. *Dead!* It can't be possible. Katherine . . . who I've gone to school with, been friends—and enemies—with. My stomach hiccups spasmodically and I taste bile burning the back of my throat. I can't believe that this is happening, that I've just touched a dead person, someone I know, someone my own age.

Someone . . . who's just been murdered.

The hot bile surges up into my throat again and I manage to swallow it back. Despite the cool autumn air, perspiration breaks out on my forehead and I feel its dampness on my skin. The slightest wisps of moonlight trickle down through the branches overhead, which cast shadows on Katherine's blood-mottled face. The light illuminates the horrible deep red slashes in her soft pale skin. Her eyes are open, blank, unseeing. I can't look at them.

Something, barely a glint in the dark, is lying on the ground beside her. I reach for it. A knife. The handle is wet, but this wetness has a different feel than water. Thicker, and both slipperier and stickier at the same time. I look down at the blade, blotched with blood, and can just make out near the handle a brand logo of two white stick-figure men against a square red background. Unwanted thoughts invade my brain—the horrible image of the blade slicing into Katherine's soft flesh. I feel my stomach churn again, the bile threatening to rise. I swallow hard, forcing it back.

Through the trees, footsteps approach, rustling the brush and branches. People are coming. I feel their shadows looming over me, and I look up at their dark silhouettes.

"You killed her!" That sounds like Dakota's voice.

What! The words startle like an unexpected punch. "No! What are you talking about? That's not what happened!"

"Why'd you do it?" another voice demands. In the shadows behind the dugout, there's a small crowd now. Their dark faces are a blur.

"You know why," Dakota answers before I can even think of what to say.

There's a burst of light. Someone's taken a picture with a cell phone. I look down at the bloody knife in my hand. *Oh no!*

Fear floods through me and I drop it. *I didn't do anything!* Just moments ago at the kegger, Dakota told me Katherine had disappeared, and said I should go look for her by the baseball dugout.

There's another flash. I spring to my feet, wiping my bloody hands on my jeans. How could they think I'd do such a thing? How could anyone do this to anyone?

"Call the cops," Dakota says.

"No!" I cry. "I mean, yes! You have to call them. But not because of me! I just found her here. I swear!"

People mutter. There's another flash. I take a step back. They can't be serious. They can't really believe I'd—

"Don't let her go," Dakota cautions.

"But I didn't do it!" I blurt.

"God, look who's talking," someone says.

"Do you believe it?" says Dakota. "Of all the people?"

The words pierce. Everyone knows why she's saying that. Because it's happened before. This is the second time in my life I've been this close to a bloodied, battered body. The second time I've seen the carnage one person can do to another. Suddenly it's obvious they're never going to believe me. Not in a million years.

"Don't let her go!" Dakota says with more urgency as I back farther from the body.

Panic-stricken, I turn and dive into the dark, running as fast as I can, crashing through the brush, slapping branches out of the way, stumbling on rocks, my face and arms being scratched by things I can't see.

"Get her!" Dakota yells, only now her voice is more distant.

* * *

They say I always ran. From the time I could walk. It was almost like I went straight from crawling to running. I was the kid in the hall the teachers were always telling to slow down, the one who'd run even when there was no rush. I'm little, only four foot ten and ninety-eight pounds. Coach Reynolds, who's in charge of the cross-country team, once told me he'd seen my type before. Small girls who could run forever. I didn't like being thought of as a "type," but there was some truth to it. I used to see other girls like me at meets. But I'd wonder if they ran for the same reason I did. In my family, it was a matter of survival.

chapter 2

Saturday 11:53 P.M.

I COME OUT of the woods, then dash across Seaver Street and into the Glen. The houses here are big old Tudors with spires, white stucco walls, and leaded windows. My heart is banging in my chest, from both running and fear. Slowing to a jog and weaving away from the bright spots under the streetlights, I know I have to find a place to stop and think. Finally, in a side yard, I see a child's playhouse. It's the size of a small shed, with a miniature porch, windows, and a door.

After tiptoeing across the lawn, I gently step onto the little porch and carefully, slowly, pull open the door, hoping it won't squeak. I'm praying that the people who own this property don't have a dog that will start barking. It's dark inside, but with the door open I can make out a small yellow plastic table and two red plastic child-size chairs. I let the door close and find myself in blackness. Can't see my hands in front of my face. But it's oddly reassuring. If I can't see myself, then no one can see me, either. I sit on one of the chairs, press my face into my hands, and take steady breaths, trying to calm down.

But my heart's still drumming and I still cannot believe what just happened. Katherine murdered?

And now what? I've never run away like that before. I never did anything wrong that would have required running. *Why did I run? Why didn't I stay and try to explain?* Because they'd see me beside Katherine's body with that bloody knife in my hand and Dakota saying, *Do you believe it? Of all the people?*

Of course they'd believe it. After all, two years ago my older brother, Sebastian, made national news by bludgeoning our father nearly to death with a two-by-four, leaving him brain damaged and mute and paralyzed from the neck down. What's so hard to believe? Like brother, like sister, right?

Into the inky stillness inside the playhouse comes the distant sound of sirens. Dread chills my veins. The police are coming. I can picture what's happening. Based on the phone calls from kids at the kegger, a code 11-41 has been issued. The boxy red-and-white ambulance is pulling out of its bay at the new town center.

The sirens grow louder and closer. The police will be the first to arrive, and they'll hurry across the baseball field and into the woods with flashlights. The kids will show them Katherine's body behind the dugout and tell them what they saw . . . *Callie Carson kneeling beside the body with a knife in her hand . . .*

But the officers have a more urgent matter. One will check Katherine's vital signs while the other scrambles back to the patrol car for the medical kit. Maybe, having seen the body, they already know it's too late—only when a kid's life is involved, it's never too late. They have to try no matter what. Maybe she's still clinging to life. Maybe they can manage a miracle.

The officer with the medical kit returns. He and his partner make a valiant but vain attempt to revive Katherine. Moments later the ambulance crew arrives. The EMTs hurry in and take over. Now one of the officers gets on his radio to report the grim news. Looks like a code 187 (homicide).

They will tell the kids to step back but stay close. After all, there may be a homicidal maniac on the loose. By now the detectives have arrived and surveyed the murder scene. While one looks for clues, the other takes the names and addresses of witnesses to be interviewed first thing tomorrow morning, while memories are still fresh. Based on the initial information, a BOLO will be issued before long: "Be on the lookout for Callie Carson, age seventeen, four foot ten, roughly a hundred pounds, dressed in jeans and a black hooded sweatshirt."

And here I am, maybe a quarter of a mile away, quivering in the dark with no idea of what to do.

About a year ago, Katherine Remington-Day, the most popular girl in the grade, started to be nice to me, inviting me to sit at her table at lunch and do things with her and her friends after school. The Remingtons were the town's earliest residents. Katherine's ancestors had first come to Soundview in the early 1800s. In the town hall was a row of portraits of the mayors going back to the 1820s, and close to half a dozen had the last name Remington.

Katherine was a dynamo, maybe three inches taller than me, with a light brown pageboy haircut and mad-crazy amounts of energy. No one else was on more committees or involved in more school activities, even though she did avoid any position that required an election. When she made it clear that she wanted to be friends, I figured I was just a charity case to her. Sometimes, in a dark moment, I even wondered if she was using me to prove just how powerful and popular she was. Powerful enough that she could have the loser Callie Carson as a friend and still be the center of the social swirl.

But the reason didn't matter. I was desperate for distraction, for friends in school, for a little fun. My family had been irreparably fractured. I'd quit the cross-country team just when it looked like we had a chance to win the statewide championship. My boyfriend, Slade, was working long hours, sometimes on jobs out of town, and my best friend, Jeanie, had moved back to England. And out of nowhere, there was Katherine, offering me a lifeline. I had to believe that anyone in my situation would have leaped to take it.

chapter 3

Sunday 12:08 A.M.

THE SIRENS HAVE stopped. By now Katherine's body has been photographed, and the murder weapon slid carefully into a small plastic bag to be examined at the police lab. The EMTs will transport the body to the morgue for autopsy. The detectives will leave, knowing that early in the morning they will return to inspect the scene of the crime in the daylight, and then interview the witnesses.

No, wait, something else will happen first. In fact, it could be happening right now. The doorbell at my house will ring. My mother, in bed, will open her eyes and groggily fumble for the light. Dulled and foggy-headed from sleeping pills and merlot, she'll be uncertain whether the doorbell really rang or she only dreamt it. But the bell will ring again and now alarm will begin to creep into the outer edges of her thoughts as she wonders who has awakened her at this hour. She will pull on her robe, but before she goes to see who is at the door, she will check on Dad to make sure he's still breathing, and she will peek into my bedroom to see if I'm home.

And when she sees that my bed is empty, her alarm will leap closer to panic.

A police officer, or perhaps a detective, will be at the door. At the sight of him, Mom will struggle to retain some semblance of calm. He will want to know if I'm home, and when she says no, he will want to know if she's heard from me tonight. Filled with foreboding, she will shake her head and ask, *Why, what's happened?* I don't know if the officer or detective will tell her about Katherine. But I do know that he will say that the police are looking for me and that my mother should be in touch with them as soon as she sees or hears from me.

Mom will ask why again. Now that I think of it, the police officer will probably tell her: there's been a murder.

Katherine was a snob and proud of it. She was judgmental and sometimes mean and cruel. She believed in good grammar and manners and was quick to correct your mistakes. Even though she herself was sort of plain, she was contemptuous of slovenly dress. Some people disliked her and some were afraid of her, but most agreed that she was a force in our school.

At first when she took me under her wing, it was a huge relief. Suddenly I'd gone from the bleakest, lowest point ever to having something to look forward to every day. Sitting at lunch, listening to Katherine and the others gab, knowing I'd be invited to go to movies, the mall, and slumber parties. It almost seemed like a miracle.

The other thing is you can tell yourself you're a charity case without really believing it. And then the day comes when you forget. And you think you really do belong. Because you want to so badly.

"Go slap David Sloan in the face," Katherine told Mia Flom one day at lunch. Mia was one of the girls Katherine allowed to sit at the table, but at the far end. She was blonde and slightly chubby, and depending on how and when you saw her, sometimes she looked pretty and sometimes she didn't. She was a reporter for the school newspaper and had a flair for writing. As far as I could tell, she was a nice girl who most people liked. She easily could have had a group of friends who accepted and enjoyed her, but instead, she seemed absolutely determined to break into Katherine's group.

"Why?" Mia asked, clearly startled.

"Because I said so," replied Katherine, delivering the line dramatically and with inflection, as if she were an actress. Of course, she wasn't an actress. She would never put herself in a position where she could be judged or criticized.

The other girls had stopped talking. Within Katherine's crowd there seemed to be two subgroups—those who were close to Katherine and those who wished they were closer. I'm not speaking of proximity alone. First came Dakota Jenkins, the daughter of Congresswoman Cynthia Jenkins. Katherine whispered to and seemed to confide in her more than anyone else. That is, if they weren't fighting, which they did a lot. Next came Zelda McDowell, whose family was said to be the richest in town, and Jodie Peters, who you sometimes saw in ads on TV. And then came the rest, down at the other end of the table, three or four

11

girls who, like Mia, were always trying to get Katherine's attention and approval.

"What are you waiting for?" Katherine asked.

Mia's eyes darted toward a group of boys standing nearby, talking and shooting occasional glances in our direction as if they knew, or hoped, that we were aware of them. David Sloan was the tallest, and probably most handsome, of the group. The previous Friday he had been Katherine's date to a Sadie Hawkins dance, and there'd been rumors that they'd vanished together into a bedroom during a party on the following night.

Mia got up stiffly and started in David's direction. Halfway there she shot an uncertain glance back at Katherine, who flicked her wrist as if shooing her forward.

The boys quieted as Mia approached, taking timid steps, as if she were making her way across a pond covered by thinning ice. Finally she stopped in front of David, who, with dipping eyebrows and one side of his mouth turned up, looked both skeptical and amused. The boys around them were silent. Mia reached up and "slapped" David's face. It was barely more than a tap. Then, her face much redder than his, she scurried back toward us.

David looked in our direction, his eyes not on Mia but on Katherine. He shoved his fists in his pockets, nodded slightly, and smirked, as if he understood precisely why she had sent a minion to deliver the faux blow. Katherine nodded back, then turned to the table just as Mia sat down, still red-faced and breathing hard.

"You call that a slap?" Katherine said, then ignored Mia for the rest of lunch.

* * *

"How does she do it? I mean, manage to instill so much fear?"

"By being judgmental and having a wicked tongue. It's a lethal combination."

"Only if people care."

"Some do; some don't."

"I'd so like to put her in her place."

"Ha! See?"

"See what?"

"You wouldn't say that if you didn't care."

Sunday 12:15 A.M.

THE POLICE OFFICER will leave. My mother will shut the door and press her back against it to keep her from collapsing to the floor. She will be devastated—in the first moments of being ravaged by emotional turmoil. But of all the possible emotions, the one she will not feel is shock. At this point, there's nothing left that can surprise her.

In the playhouse the air is musty and smells like dry wood. I can't help thinking of the children who have played in here. Little girls serving pretend meals to dolls seated around the table. Boys kneeling at the windows, firing toy guns at imaginary attackers. But here in the dark now, there is nothing pretend or imaginary. It's all horribly real.

My cell phone vibrates. With trembling fingers I pull it out of my pocket. It's Mom.

"Are the police there?" I ask.

"They just left." Her voice is high and anxious. "A murder? My God, Cal, what's going on?"

My heart heaves and my eyes become watery. As frightened as I am, I feel even worse for her. After everything she's been through. Sebastian and Dad. And now this? It's as if her family is slowly being destroyed before her eyes.

Tears spill out and roll down my cheeks. "I didn't do it," I manage to croak. "I only found her after she'd been stabbed."

"Where are you?"

"I'm . . ." I hesitate, knowing how she'll react. "Hiding."

"*What?* Why?" Predictably, her voice rises even higher. "Go to the police. Tell them you didn't kill her."

I can't bring myself to explain about my picking up the knife and the photos they took. Or about the troubles between Katherine and me that I never told Mom about. "They won't believe me." I sniff miserably, feeling another wave of emotion rising inside me. "I can't explain now. Just . . . check under the umbrella."

"What?"

"You'll figure it out. I have to go. Don't call back."

I snap the phone shut.

Almost instantly it rings again.

It's my mother, of course.

But instead of answering, I burst into sobs.

My brother, Sebastian, is four years older than me. As far back as I can remember, Dad wanted him to be a professional athlete. While some sons obediently tried to live up to their fathers' wishes, Sebastian stubbornly refused. It got so bad they even went to a psychologist, who said that the best thing

Dad could do was back off and let Sebastian be.

But Dad could no more back off than Sebastian could be obedient. They were polar forces, feeding off each other's determination. From the start there was violence. As Sebastian grew older, spankings by hand gave way to spankings by paddle, which gave way to slaps, punches, then all-out fistfights. Mom and I were stunned into silence by the poisonous brutality between them. People at school noticed Sebastian's bruises. Social services got involved. A few times the police were called. Neighbors gossiped. Rumors spread. People around town began to avoid us. Mom sank inward and became depressed and withdrawn.

I ran.

chapter 5

Sunday 12:25 A.M.

I TAKE DEEP breaths, dry my eyes, and try to think about what I have to do next. The phone vibrates. It's my mother again. But she can't help. Most of the time she's so overwhelmed she can barely take care of Dad.

There's only one other person I'm certain will believe me. But the last time we spoke, I broke his heart. I could blame Katherine for that. But she didn't make that phone call; I did.

"I think we should make some that look like boobs," Katherine said one afternoon last February when we were at Dakota's house making cookies for the Spirit Day bake sale. Dakota, then the student council vice president, was planning to run for president in senior year.

The rest of us giggled. Katherine, who came off as so proper, could always make us laugh when she said something outrageous.

"Well, I mean, the idea is to sell a lot of cookies, right?" Katherine said.

"The boys would love it," I said.

"Some of the girls, too," said Jodie, who was mixing dough with Dakota in the big white KitchenAid mixer.

"I'm sure Mr. Carter would be thrilled," said Dakota.

"Mean old man," Katherine muttered.

"No way," Dakota said. "He gave Seth Phillips and I a—"

"Seth Phillips and *me*," Katherine quickly corrected her.

Dakota rolled her eyes. "He gave Seth Phillips and me permission to skip gym when we needed to work on PACE."

PACE was the performing arts program at our school.

"And he made a special arrangement so that Slade could get out of school early and help his dad," I added.

"Ah, Slade." Katherine looked at her watch. "Gee, Callie, it's been almost fifteen minutes since you brought him up. By the way, has he heard from Harvard or Yale?"

It was hard to know sometimes whether she was being serious or just kidding around. She knew he wasn't going to college. At the counter, Dakota and Jodie were silent. I could feel the mood shift from one of gaiety and laughter to something else. This, too, happened often.

"He's going into the National Guard," I said. "And when he gets back from training, he'll work in his dad's business."

"Construction?" Katherine said with a disapproving wrinkle of her nose. This wasn't the first time she'd been critical of Slade, and I really didn't like it. It felt like she was putting me in the position of having to decide between them. At first, when she'd invited me into her crowd, it had all been fun and laughs. I'd come to relish times like this, when I was included here in

Dakota's kitchen with Katherine's closest friends, knowing that Mia and the other far-end-of-the-table girls would have died to be in my place. But along with that growing familiarity came a feeling of vulnerability: I had become an unprotected target should Katherine decide to hurl her pointed opinions in my direction.

I looked down at the cookie sheet and busied myself pressing green sugar letters into the dough, spelling out "Go Tigers," "Win," and "Tiger Pride!" Not only did Slade work with his father in construction but they'd also helped renovate that very kitchen.

I remembered Slade telling me that it was the biggest kitchen he'd ever seen. It seemed like it had acres of dark green marble countertops, punctuated by dual sinks, brushed-steel appliances, and a large iron ring suspended from the ceiling with a dozen pots and pans hanging from it. Slade had said it had been one of those jobs for which money wasn't an issue. The Jenkinses had wanted everything to be perfect.

Just when I thought the topic of Slade had been dropped, Jodie said, "How long have you two been together?"

"Three years," I answered.

"So . . . you've never been with anyone else?" Jodie was a funny girl, with short hair and a bouncy personality and a wicked sense of humor when she felt like displaying it.

I shook my head.

"How can you know if he's the one for you?" she asked. "I mean, when you've had no one else to compare him to."

"I just do," I said, and thought, *I don't need to compare him to anyone else.*

"I think you could do so much better," Katherine declared.

My ears burned. This was something else I'd learned about Katherine. Sometimes she'd get into moods and had to stir things up, cause excitement, and push buttons. She was like a school-yard bully who couldn't resist picking fights. But unlike some bullies, who picked fights only with kids they knew they could beat, Katherine seemed to have this need to create confrontations even when the outcome was uncertain.

I could have reacted to what she'd said about Slade, could have gotten angry or more defensive, even argued. I think Katherine actually liked it better when you fought back than when you meekly obeyed her, the way Mia always did. But instead, I decided to try a strategy based on something my father used to say: *A good offense is the best defense.*

"Tell me, Katherine, have *you* ever been in love?" I asked.

Dakota and Jodie froze like meerkats on TV. Katherine conjured up a haughty "Ha!" but after that, the kitchen fell uncomfortably quiet again. I was tempted to push Katherine on the question—after all, "ha" didn't exactly qualify as an answer—but I sensed I'd gone far enough. I'd stood up to the queen and silenced her.

Katherine glanced around and her gaze stopped at a block of wood containing a set of kitchen knives. Her hand closed around the largest handle and she drew out a long, heavy-looking blade and held it in my direction for a moment in a way that could have been either innocent or threatening. The mood in the kitchen was ominous. Even though what Katherine was doing was a teasing gesture, there was something menacing about it.

Staring at the knife, I noticed the design on the side of the blade—two tiny white stick figures against a square red background.

Katherine turned toward me. Dakota and Jodie could see what she was doing, but they couldn't see her expression change from a chatty smile to an intensely unamused glare. Suddenly she jabbed the knife forward, not nearly enough to reach me, but enough to make me jump back.

"Aaah!" Jodie gasped, as if she really thought Katherine was going to stab me.

Katherine turned and smiled at her. "You didn't think I'd do it, did you?"

A nervous grin appeared on Jodie's face, while Dakota's remained a mask. Katherine slid the knife back into the block and gazed at me again, nodding slightly. I couldn't help interpreting the act as a serious warning not to overstep my boundaries.

chapter 6

CAN I BRING myself to call Slade now, after what I did to him? And I did it in the worst possible way and at the worst possible time. He was at National Guard training camp, far from home, his friends, and family. Farther away than he'd ever gone alone.

For the first two months he'd been allowed only one three-minute phone call—to tell his dad he'd made it to the training camp safely. After that, he was allowed to speak to me once a week. He'd confide about how lonely and miserable he was, about how scared he was of being called up for active duty and sent overseas, and about how much he regretted signing up for the guard in the first place. These were things he never could have admitted to anyone else. But he could say them to me, because he trusted me. At least, until I betrayed him.

Pangs of regret surge through me, but they're nothing new. I've been feeling them ever since we broke up. Slade's been home from Guard training for nearly a week. I've seen his pickup at the new town center. He's working there with his father to get everything ready for the opening celebration. I've been so tempted to call and tell him how sorry I am. But how would I answer when he asked the inevitable question: why did I do it?

How could I tell him? How can I face him?

He'd be completely entitled to tell me to go to hell. After all, that was basically what I did when he was alone and needy.

And yet I don't think he will. He's a better person than that.

I call. As it rings, I feel myself growing tense and my heart revving up. Then that strange mixture of disappointment and relief when I get his answering message. I swallow and begin: "Slade, please call me. It's urgent, a matter of life and death. I wouldn't bother you otherwise, but something terrible's happened. I know you probably hate me and never want to hear from me again, but you're the only person I can trust. *Please* call me as soon as you can!"

I close the phone and wait for my heart to slow. But my emotions are a hurricane of yearning, regret, need, and fear. Just hearing his voice on the message brings fresh tears to my eyes.

Slade doesn't call back. It seems like at least half an hour has passed, but when I check the time, it's only been ten minutes. He could be at the movies, at a party, anywhere. And with anyone. Even now, in the middle of all this, that's the thought I hate most.

I call again, leave another message. I imagine him listening to the first message and thinking I can drop dead. He owes me nothing. But maybe the second message will make him reconsider.

I wait in the dark. Seconds feel like minutes, and minutes feel like forever. It's agony to imagine him listening to my messages and being unmoved. But what did I think would happen? Did I think he'd come back from Guard training brokenhearted and sit by the phone every night waiting for me to call and say I'd made a mistake and I was sorry?

In your dreams, Callie Carson.

I know it makes no sense to keep calling and leaving messages, but I can't help myself. I call again, knowing there's probably nothing I can do or say to change his mind, but feeling like I have to try anyway.

"Slade, please, I . . ." There's a catch in my throat as tears well up in my eyes. I've cried so much tonight that they're raw and sore. "I'm so sorry to put this on you, really I am. I know I was awful to you. But you don't know how much I regret what I did. I mean, even before this . . . this horrible thing that happened tonight. I was sorry, but I didn't know what to say. I didn't know how to tell you I'd made a terrible mistake. I felt like I'd already hurt you so bad that it wouldn't be fair. But I . . . I . . ."

What I want to say is that I still love him, but it's too much all at once. Some protective instinct deep inside won't allow me to reveal that much or leave myself that vulnerable, even if it's been all I've felt for weeks and has nothing to do with what happened tonight.

I've always loved him.

I close the phone. Three messages is enough. Salty tears sting my raw cheeks.

"Here's to rapid metabolisms," Jodie toasted one afternoon in late

March when she, Zelda, Katherine, and I were in the city. She raised her s'more cupcake and we joined in.

"Rue the day these go straight to our thighs," Zelda declared.

"Hear! Hear!" Katherine chimed in. It was one of those periods when she and Dakota weren't speaking. We never knew why the two of them ran so hot and cold. But they were like the weather: all you had to do was wait and everything would change.

Before Katherine, I'd never gone to the city without an adult, but now we went practically every other weekend, and always to some special place she knew about. That day we were in the Magnolia Bakery.

"What say ye, sweet Callie?" Katherine asked.

"This is definitely the most delicious thing I've ever tasted," I said, licking the creamy icing off a cupcake called a Hummingbird.

"Easy to say for someone who's probably only had Hostess Twinkies," Katherine quipped. The smiles fell off the other girls' faces as they waited to see if I'd rise to the dig or let it pass. I decided to take the middle road.

"We can't all be gourmands, like you," I said with a somewhat forced smile.

"You mean 'gourmet,'" she replied with a dismissive roll of her eyes. "A gourmand is an indiscriminant eater."

"Ooh, look who remembers all that vocabulary we learned for our SATs," Jodie teased in a way that I suspected was meant to defuse the situation.

"I am *so* happy that's over with," Zelda groaned, and turned to me. "So what are your plans for after high school, Callie?"

I assumed she'd meant the question in a genuine way, to change the subject. But unfortunately it was one I'd been trying to avoid. I hoped I'd go to Fairchester Community College, which I hoped we'd be able to afford with the help of financial aid. I was a pretty good student and had been a pretty good cross-country runner, but didn't excel at either enough to deserve any kind of scholarship. But the prevailing attitude in Katherine's crowd was that community college was for losers. So I answered her question with "I don't know."

"I wish I could be like that," Jodie said with a wistful sigh.

"Like what?" I asked uncertainly.

"Just not having to worry," she said. "I mean, about the future."

I was about to argue that I did have to worry about the future, but then I caught myself. She was right. I wasn't that worried about the *future*. I was too caught up in the present—busy thinking about Slade's recent announcement that he'd signed up for the Army National Guard and would leave on May 21 for three months of training, and wondering whether my mother could cope with taking care of my father, and whether there was still a way to appeal the judge's decision that had put my brother in prison for eight to fifteen years.

"You know, maybe if you were with the right kind of guy . . . ," Katherine said, then pretended to catch herself. "I mean, maybe if you were with a *different* kind of guy . . . Someone more goal oriented."

"Slade is goal oriented," I said.

"Oh, yes," Katherine said, dabbing some white cream

filling off her lip with a napkin. "Construction."

"Drywall," I said. "It's what's in most houses and buildings unless they're really old. Slade and his dad install it."

"Manual labor," Katherine said with a snarky and superior little smile. It was one of those moments when another girl might have backed down and pretended to ignore the insult. But I resented the insinuation.

"It's honest work," I said, jutting my chin forward.

Katherine's eyes sharpened, and she leaned toward me, as if accepting the challenge. "No one said it wasn't."

For a moment we stared at each other as if it were a contest. Katherine was right. No one had said that what Slade and his father did wasn't honest work, but she'd made it obvious that she thought it was the sort of honest work only a moron would do.

"I'm just curious," I said. "What does *your* father do?"

A pall swept over our table. Zelda stared down at her caramel-meringue cupcake, and Jodie suddenly seemed fascinated by the pedestrians passing. Katherine gazed at me, appearing unruffled, although I thought I detected a tic under her left eye.

"He's"—she hesitated, then continued—"between jobs."

I was just about to ask her how long her father had been unemployed when Zelda suddenly said, "Katherine's family is in real estate."

There was nothing wrong with being unemployed. It happened to lots of people. But it certainly didn't put Katherine in a position from which she could look down on people who were at least doing something, even if it did involve—God forbid—manual labor.

chapter 7

Sunday 1:05 A.M.

MOM HAS GIVEN up trying to reach me. Slade either hasn't gotten my messages or has decided to ignore them. So now what? I can't hide in this playhouse forever. What am I going to do? How am I going to fight this? There is no way I'm going to turn myself in, like Mom suggested. I saw what almost happened to my brother thanks to an inexperienced public defender. You may be innocent until proven guilty, but sometimes you're guilty in people's minds long before you set foot in a courtroom.

And I will *not* allow that to happen to me, or to my mother, or to what little is left of our family.

The phone vibrates. I flip it open and look at the number. It's Slade! My heart leaps.

"Where are you?" he asks.

Oh my God! How many nights have I cried myself to sleep, yearning to hear his voice? I try to answer his question, but what comes out is a choked gurgle followed by sobs as I'm overwhelmed by a flood of feelings.

"Cal?" Slade says.

"I . . . I . . . Just give me a minute." I try to catch my breath and calm myself. I'm happy and sad and scared and stressed. "Just don't hang up. I have to talk to you. Don't go away."

"I won't."

I have to focus, get ahold of myself, stop trembling, breathe steadily. Finally I feel like I can speak again. "Thank you for calling me back. I know you didn't have to. You probably didn't even want to. I'm so sorry for what I did, Slade. You don't know how many times I wanted to tell you. And now you probably never want to see me again."

"No, that's not true," he says, but his voice is clenched like a fist.

Still, that's all it takes for my filter to fall away and allow me to blurt, "I still love you."

First there's silence. Then he says, "Don't say that, Cal."

It would have been better if I hadn't told him so soon, but now it's too late. There's no backing away. "Slade, I want to explain why I broke up with you. It was such a stupid, idiotic reason, and I've regretted it every second since. But I don't have time now. Because . . . you won't believe what happened tonight. Slade, I need to talk to you. I need your help. I . . . I—" When I think about the enormity of the task I'm faced with, tears start to bubble up and the shaking returns.

"Okay, stay calm," he says. "Take a breath and tell me where you are."

I do what he says and feel the cool air fill my lungs before I exhale. "Up in the Glen. In someone's yard. In a kids' playhouse."

"What street?"

"I don't know. The first one on the right when you drive in. A couple of houses down. I'm so sorry, Slade. I've wanted to tell you for so long. I just wish it didn't have to be like this. Please, believe me."

"Cal, I can't—" he begins, his voice suddenly anguished. I hear something bang in the background; then he curses under his breath.

"What is it, Slade?"

He ignores the question. "I'm coming. Just promise you won't go anywhere, okay? Just be there when I get there."

A surge of grateful relief floods through me. "I will, I promise. Thank you so much."

We met at a football game when I was in eighth grade. I'd never been to a high-school game before, and my friends and I thought it would be daring and exciting to sit in the stands with the older kids.

At one point my best friend, Jeanie, and I decided to go get something to drink. Neither she nor I was a big football fan, and thus far, we'd been underwhelmed by what we'd seen. The snack bar was across the field and Jeanie suggested we cut across rather than walk all the way around.

"I don't think we should," I said.

"Oh, come on, don't be a wanker," she said, using one of her funny British words. "They're all the way down at the other end. Everyone's looking that way. They probably wouldn't even notice us."

I agreed reluctantly, but no sooner did we set foot on the field than a blond guy standing with some people near an EMS truck waved and shouted at us: "Hey! Get off the field!" While I hesitated, Jeanie, who had been experimenting lately with bold rebelliousness, said to ignore him and keep going. Meanwhile, the guy started jogging toward us, still waving his arms.

"Hey! You can't just walk on the field!" he called.

"Yes, we can," Jeanie called back. "They're all down the other way."

"One loose ball and they could be on top of you in an instant," he yelled.

I started to jog off the field. Jeanie made a big show of rolling her eyes and then began strolling slowly, clearly letting him know that she was going to take her time. Just then a loud roar came from the crowd and we turned to see a horde of brutes in helmets and jerseys stampeding toward us. The one in the lead had the ball cradled in his arms.

In a flash, Jeanie and I were running for our lives. We'd just gotten off the field when the roar turned to cheers and the ball carrier crossed the goal line not ten feet behind us.

"See?" The blond guy chuckled and grinned. He had nice teeth and a thin but athletic build. "What are you, like fifth graders or something?"

Jeanie was medium-size and slender. But I knew that the reason he'd asked was that I was so small. "Beg your pardon," Jeanie huffed with annoyance, and pointed at the brick high-school building. "We'll be here next year."

"Oh, yeah?" The blond guy looked surprised, and I couldn't

help noticing that his gaze was mostly on me. "That really true?"

I nodded.

"Okay, Shrimp, see you next year."

I might have minded being called shrimp if I hadn't been so used to it. Jeanie and I got our drinks at the snack bar, and to be honest, I didn't give any more thought to the blond guy, who was obviously older and no doubt dated older girls.

But later, after the game, my friends and I passed the EMS truck, and there he was. Our eyes met and I had the strangest feeling that he'd been waiting for me.

"Enjoy the game?" he asked.

"Not really," I answered truthfully. Our eyes stayed on each other.

"Hey," he said, "you guys want to see what the inside of an EMS truck looks like?"

My girlfriends and I shared curious looks. None of us cared about the truck, but we were all interested in attractive older boys, especially the ones who paid attention to us. The blond guy opened the back of the truck and pointed out the stretcher and medical kits and oxygen tanks.

"What's the oxygen for?" I asked.

He seemed glad that I'd asked. "Smoke inhalation," he said. "For people in fires. Firefighters, too. They get overcome by smoke."

"Have *you* ever saved anyone?" asked a girl named Mary.

"I'm not old enough to be an EMT, but my dad's the captain of the squad, so I get to hang around with them."

A moment later a man came around behind the truck. "Close it up, Slade, we're leaving."

Slade said he had to go, and my friends and I headed home.

"He likes you," Jeanie said to me as soon as we were out of earshot.

"How do you know?" I asked, even though inside I was thrilled, as this confirmed that it wasn't all in my imagination.

"You could tell," she said.

A few days later Slade was outside on the sidewalk after school. He asked if he could walk with me. Even though he was two years older, he had an easy, relaxed way that wasn't threatening. He was there the next day and the next, and soon we were texting and calling and doing things together.

A month later we were boyfriend and girlfriend. I was the only girl at Soundview Middle School who was seeing a sophomore from the high school. To me it didn't matter how old Slade was, but a lot of my classmates were in awe.

chapter 8

Sunday 1:13 A.M.

MY PHONE VIBRATES. It's Slade. I leave the playhouse and sprint across the yard and to the street. A pair of headlights is rolling slowly toward me. I grab the passenger-side door and get in. Slade starts to drive. I'm too overwhelmed to speak. Overwhelmed by what's happened, overwhelmed by suddenly being close to him, by again sitting in this seat where I spent so much time when we used to drive to parties and keggers and secret hiding places.

"Thank you so much," I manage to croak.

"It's okay." He's got alcohol on his breath. It's not surprising for a Saturday night, but should he be driving? I'm in no position to ask. The memory of Katherine's body keeps coming back. Knowing her, I'd suspect that it was a ruse, a nasty trick. But it wasn't. I felt for her pulse; I saw those wounds and all that blood. Unless it's some kind of crazy dream I'll wake up from at any moment, it's real. I take a deep breath and force myself back to Slade.

"I . . . I meant everything I said on the phone."

He doesn't respond. Doesn't look at me. Just drives.

So I tell him what happened tonight. How I found Katherine.

"You picked up the knife?" he asks, surprised.

"It was dark and I wasn't sure what it was, and the next thing I knew, they were taking pictures. . . ."

"Of you holding the knife?"

"Uh-huh." And I tell him how I thought of Sebastian and what everyone was bound to think and how Dakota said to call the police and I got scared and ran away. "That's when I called you. I didn't know what else to do. What do *you* think I should do?"

He's quiet for a moment, then says, "Go to the police, Cal. Tell them what happened."

"They'll never believe me."

"You don't know that."

"After what happened with my brother? And with my fingerprints on the knife? Are you serious?" I feel myself getting worked up.

"Calm down," Slade says.

I take a deep breath. We ride along in the dark, and thank God he's driving straight and at a steady speed. I don't know where we're going, but I know why he wants me to turn myself in. Because he's honest and forthright and does the things you're supposed to do.

"I won't stand a chance. It'll kill my mom. I can't do that to her."

Ahead, a police car with flashing lights screeches around a corner and races toward us. Panic seizes me and I duck below the dashboard and watch the red and blue lights illuminate the inside of the pickup's cab. The police car zooms past. Back in the seat, my pulse still racing, I tell Slade, "We can't drive around like this. People know about us. It won't be long before the police start looking for you."

He drums his fingers against the steering wheel. We go over a bump and the pickup rattles. I flinch, impatient and jumpy. This is a small suburban town and I feel like we're a moving target. "Talk to me, Slade. Tell me what you're thinking."

Keeping his eyes straight ahead, he says, "You said you wanted to explain why you broke up with me."

"I do, but not driving around like this. Make a left, okay?"

"The old EMS building?"

"Uh-huh."

Just before the bridge over the train tracks, Slade turns into a driveway. The ride gets bumpy. The asphalt has broken up and there are ruts and potholes. Ahead is the old EMS building, empty now that emergency services has been transferred to the new town center.

Slade drives to a far corner of the parking lot, where trees block the moonlight and it's almost as dark as it was in the playhouse. I lower the window and hear the distant hum of traffic from the thruway. Across the lot the old EMS building is dark and empty. Sometimes Slade and I hung out there with the EMS crew, playing pool or just talking and passing the time.

Cool night air drifts in through the open window. Slade is waiting for my story.

"What about Alex Craft?" Katherine asked one day at lunch. It seemed like the more I resisted her suggestion that I could find a better boyfriend, the more intent she became on proving it.

I rolled my eyes at her. A hush rippled through the other girls at the table. No one else dared roll her eyes at Katherine the Great. But while she might have beheaded another girl for it, Katherine tolerated it from me. Almost as if she knew that the more I needed her approval, the more I had to demonstrate my independence.

"Brianna, go ask Alex if he'd like to go out with Callie," Katherine said to one of the far-end-of-the-table girls.

"Don't," I said, but Brianna was already rising. She was new at school that year, wore her long black hair in a ponytail, and was tall and athletic and played on the girls' basketball team. But despite her size, she was quiet and unassuming, and sometimes you almost forgot she was there.

As Brianna started across the cafeteria to the table where Alex sat with some friends, I pretended to be embarrassed. But to be honest, I was a little curious. Alex was a major cutie. Not that I would ever go out with him. Everyone knew my heart belonged to Slade. But just the same, all of us watched. All of us, that is, except Katherine. I glanced in her direction and discovered that she was watching me, and that she'd no doubt seen the curious, almost excited, anticipation on my face as I waited to see how Alex would respond. Now instead of faking embarrassment, I truly did feel my cheeks grow hot as I realized that the whole thing had nothing to do with how Alex might answer, and everything to do with how I felt about his being asked.

Sunday 1:36 A.M.

IN THE PICKUP I've just finished telling Slade about how Katherine relentlessly worked on me, how it seemed to have become her personal mission to get me to break up with him, how foolishly dazzled I was by the life she was offering, how it got to the point where I felt like I had to choose between her and him. And Katherine was there every day, while he was far away.

"It was just a sick game to her, Slade. Seeing if she could get people to do whatever she wanted them to. And I was scared. I was afraid you'd get called up to active duty and have to go away for years, and I didn't know how I'd manage to wait that long. Or that you'd be horribly wounded and you'd come back . . . you know . . . different."

I expect him to get angry, but instead, he nods. "Every soldier's worst nightmare."

"What is?"

"That he'll be on the other side of the world, fighting a

war that makes no sense, risking his life for his country, and the girl he's left behind won't be there for him when he comes back."

I stare into the darkness. "I heard your unit was called up."

"Yeah, but I'm not going."

"How?"

He pats his right knee. "Separation without benefits."

"What's that?"

"A week ago the medical review board DQ'd me. I'm not in the Guard anymore."

Then he won't be sent overseas! "That's great! It's fantastic!"

He just nods, tilts his head back against the headrest, and closes his eyes. Despite everything that's going on, all I've wanted to do since I got into the truck is kiss his cheek, feel his arms around me. I reach over and touch his shoulder.

"Don't!" Slade's eyes burst open. His sudden gruffness startles me and I jerk back, surprised. "It's too late!" he snaps. "I mean, you can't just say you're sorry!" He closes his eyes again and presses his forehead into his palm.

The force of his unexpected anger practically hurls me against the passenger-side door. The shock alone might have been enough to cause tears, but that's coupled with everything else that's happened, and they burst forth freely after his abrupt rejection. I don't think he's ever lost his temper with me before.

He sits with his hands tight on the steering wheel while I wipe away the tears. "But all I can do is say I'm sorry," I reply with a sniff. "I am, really. I still can't believe I did it. It's like I was under some kind of spell."

"Some other guy's spell," he mutters bitterly.

The words strike like a slap. *"What?"*

"You know." He doesn't look at me.

As if I've not already faced enough injustice for one night, now this? Indignation billows inside me. "That's so untrue! Oh my God! Who told you that?"

"Someone."

"Someone who lied. There was no one else! Ever! Not even for a second. I swear to you. Slade, you have to believe me."

He's silent. I wonder if he's weighing my words against the lie someone told him. But who would have lied to him? And why? "So who was I supposed to be seeing?"

"She didn't say."

So it's a *she* who told him. "She never said who this other guy was supposed to be?"

Slade's quiet again. Who do I know who would be capable of telling such a terrible, harmful untruth?

Katherine. Who else?

One of the far-end-of-the-table girls, Kirsten, had a mother who got us tickets to see an off-Broadway matinee called *The Children's Hour*, which wasn't anything like the title implied. Katherine and Dakota were speaking to each other again and it would be them, Zelda, Jodie, Kirsten, and me. We'd take the train to the city. Afterward Zelda's father would take us someplace to eat.

I assumed everyone was going to get dressed up for the trip. I had money from scooping ice cream and babysitting that I'd been saving for a better phone, but that could wait. I borrowed the car and went to the mall. It's embarrassing to be seventeen and still shopping for clothes in the children's department, but I managed to find a pretty green dress and shoes with heels. I used up almost all the money I'd saved.

We met on the train platform and I was shocked. The other girls were wearing jeans, as if going to the city for a show and dinner was no big deal. And I guess for them it wasn't. For a moment I felt awful. Like a real country hick who thought she had to get all fancied up for the trip to the big city. But Katherine and the other girls all rallied around me, saying how pretty I looked, how jealous they were, and how they now wished that they'd dressed up, too.

By then the train was coming and there was no time for me to go back home and change. And even though I still felt uncomfortable and out of place, I told myself that I'd done nothing wrong and there was no reason I couldn't still enjoy the outing.

We went to the show and afterward, thanks to Zelda's dad, there was a long black limo waiting for us. Everyone on the sidewalk stared as the driver held the door and we got in and rode to Whimsy, which was this incredible old-fashioned restaurant that served sliders and little plates of fries, followed by *huge* ice-cream sundaes with every topping imaginable.

It was one of the best days ever, and all the girls, including Katherine, were super nice. Then, on the train going home, I thought about how hard it would be to go back to my house, back to my depressed mom and broken dad, and to scooping ice cream every day once school ended and babysitting bratty kids most evenings. And how Slade would be going away and the only fun I could imagine having that summer would be with Katherine and her friends. I looked at Katherine, maybe expecting to see her smile and nod as if she knew what I was thinking. But she was talking to Zelda and not even looking at me. And I realized . . . this time she didn't have to look at me to know.

chapter 10

Sunday 1:47 A.M.

IN THE TRUCK I nervously pick at the old duct tape that covers the split in the passenger seat and gaze at the EMS building. Slade's still staring straight ahead. There's one thing I have to say. It comes out in a whisper: "There was never, ever, anyone else, Slade. I need you to believe that."

A long breath rushes out of his lips and he bends forward until his forehead touches the steering wheel. "What are you going to do?"

"I . . . have to figure out who the real killer is."

"How?"

I think back to tonight's events, beginning with the kegger. Mia had called and asked me to go with her. I didn't want to. I was still a little mad at her for what had happened with the story we had written together for the school newspaper. And I thought I'd be really uncomfortable if I ran into Katherine. But Mia had practically insisted. "Don't worry. Lots of people like you, Callie. And they'll be there, too. I don't even think Katherine is coming."

But of course Katherine was there.

"Cal?" Slade says, bringing me back from these thoughts.

"I'm just trying to figure it out. I'm wondering if it could have been a setup. If the whole thing could have been planned to make it look like I killed her."

"Or it just could have been some sicko passing through," Slade says. "It was in the woods, in the middle of the night. It could have been anyone. Don't you think that's a lot more likely than some high-school kids planning a murder?"

"It may have been just one high-school kid."

"Look, I know a lot of people didn't like Katherine," he says. "But why would anyone want to *kill* her? You're talking about Soundview. There hasn't been a murder here in ten years."

And only one attempted murder . . . by my brother, I can't help thinking bitterly.

Slade leans back into the shadows. I can't see his face clearly, can't tell what's on his mind. Maybe he's thinking I'll never be able to figure it out. Especially if at the same time the police are looking for me. Maybe he's regretting that he came to get me. Maybe he's wishing he never met me in the first place.

"I'm sorry, Slade. I shouldn't have gotten you involved, and I understand why you don't want to help me. You've already done way more for me than I deserve."

In the shadows, Slade doesn't move or speak. I take a deep breath and reach for the door handle.

Slade says, "Wait."

In early May, Katherine and Dakota weren't speaking to each

other again. I'm not sure anyone at the lunch table gave it much thought. We just assumed they were having another one of their mysterious arguments. They both sat in their usual places at the table, as if neither was about to give up her position, no matter what. Both chatted and gossiped with the other girls. They just didn't talk or gossip with each other.

In fact, they didn't even look at each other.

But the next day Dakota didn't show up. We'd seen her in school that morning, but now it was lunch and she wasn't in the cafeteria. And that was how everyone knew that this fight was different.

It happened during the final weeks of rehearsal for the spring PACE show. As the days passed, the situation at lunch grew stranger. How long would Dakota stay away? How long would Katherine preside over the table pretending nothing was wrong?

"What's going on?" Mia asked me one day as we walked down the hall toward gym.

"Not a clue," I answered.

Mia had a habit of tucking her chin into her neck like a turtle when she looked at you. "Are you sure?"

"Yes. I mean, why would I know?"

"You spend more time with them," Mia said. "They invite you to do more things than the rest of us."

"Not more than Zelda and Jodie."

"Those two are in a world of their own," Mia said with a shrug. "I just wish I knew what was going on. Are you *sure* you don't know? Or are you just sworn to secrecy?"

"What?" I asked, surprised.

Even though we were in the hallway, surrounded by moving bodies and loud chatter from a dozen sources, Mia moved closer and dropped her voice. "The inner circle. Don't pretend you don't know. They make you swear an oath, right?"

chapter 11

Sunday 1:53 A.M.

"You may be my closest friend, but that doesn't mean you know everything about me."

"I know you better than you know yourself."

"I hate you when you say things like that. I'll never be like you."

"Too late. You already are."

"It was Mia who invited me to the kegger," I tell Slade in the pickup. "But it was Dakota who told me Katherine was missing and that everyone was looking for her. She even told me to check behind the dugout. And it was Dakota who led everyone else to me just moments after I found Katherine's body. And you know what the first thing she said was? 'You killed her!' But how could she have known that? It was too dark to really see. Katherine still could have been alive. I was the only one who'd checked her pulse. Do you know what that means, Slade? Dakota *already knew* that Katherine was dead. She got Mia to invite me to the kegger and told her to tell me Katherine wouldn't be there. That's why she told me to look near the dugout and then led everyone there. So it would look like I did it!"

"You think *Dakota* killed Katherine?"

"How else could she have known Katherine was dead? How could she know where to tell me to look? Why else would she wait until I'd found the body and then bring a bunch of people as witnesses? She *had* to have planned it, Slade."

He's quiet. It irks me that I don't know what he's thinking. There was a time when each of us always knew what the other was thinking. We'd finish each other's sentences.

Slade looks at the clock in his phone. "I've got work in the morning. There's still a ton to do before the dedication ceremony on Wednesday. Even then we won't be finished. But at least we'll make it look good. You know who the guest speaker is?"

There is no reason I would know, and no reason Slade would ask, unless it's obvious. "Dakota's mom?"

He nods and goes quiet and I wonder if he's just had the same thought I've had: not only is Dakota's mother a congresswoman, but her uncle, Samuel Jenkins, is the chief of police and will be in charge of the investigation into the murder of Katherine Remington-Day.

We get out of the truck and walk through the dark to the old EMS building. The air is chillier than before and even quieter now, as if the traffic on the thruway is sparser at this time of night. Slade accidentally steps into a pothole and staggers a few feet, then catches himself and bends over.

"You okay?" I ask.

"Yeah, it's just the knee." He'd torn his ACL playing

football in junior high and had to have major surgery.

"I thought that didn't happen anymore," I said. He was supposed to do special exercises to strengthen the muscles around the knee and keep it stable.

"I started feeling a lot of pain toward the end of basic."

"Basic?"

"Basic training." Slade straightens up but limps. Near the building he steps off the path, takes something from under a rock, and hands it to me: a key, cold and moist from resting in its hiding place, slightly rusted along the edges. I slide it into the keyhole and turn the knob.

Inside, the air smells musty and stale, as if no one's been there for a long time. Out of habit, I reach toward the wall for the light switch. Then I feel Slade's hand close around my arm, and instantly understand. If people saw a light coming from this abandoned place, they'd be suspicious. He reaches into his pocket and takes out a key ring with a small penlight. He aims the light at the floor, careful to keep the tiny beam from hitting the windows.

A few old chairs, a dented file cabinet, and a desk are all that remain. Everything else is gone.

"They took the old pool table?" I ask. It was such a piece of junk. Balls were always getting stuck in the gullies and the guys were constantly removing one end of the table to reach inside to free them. Finally they built a hinge for the end so they could open it whenever they needed to.

"Everyone's trying to save money," Slade says. He swivels his head around, a concerned look on his face. "I don't know about this, Cal. I mean, maybe you can hide here tonight, but what're you going to do tomorrow?"

"I have to ask you for another favor," I tell him.

Slade's face contorts unhappily. In the dim light I pull open one of the desk drawers, find a torn envelope and a pencil, and start writing a list of the things I need: Black hair dye. Scissors. Makeup. Sharpies. Deodorant. Rubbing alcohol. Cotton balls. Black lipstick and nail polish. Wire cutters. An old pair of Slade's sister's jeans, sneakers, and a gray hoodie. Even though Alyssa is five years younger than me, I'm so petite that we're practically the same size.

I give the list to Slade. With a deep frown, he scans it with the penlight, then sighs loudly and slowly shakes his head. "I don't know, Cal. I'm not sure I can do this."

"Please, Slade. I'll never tell anyone you helped me. If I get caught, I'll lie. What difference will it make?"

We stand, silent, in the dark. I wish he didn't have to leave. "Promise me you'll come back?"

"I promise."

He starts to leave, then hesitates. I'm hoping he'll change his mind and stay a little longer, but instead, he takes out his keys and works the penlight free, then gives it to me and goes. Without turning on the lights, he drives out of the parking lot.

For a long time I was untouched by all the typical teen angst about popularity. The reason? My best friend, Jeanie. Each of us was the other's protector and support system. As long as we had each other, we were immune to the new styles of handbags, boots, and all the other name-brand items deemed the must-haves of the moment.

Jeanie was rebellious and daring and had a resourceful style all her own. I'd spend hours at her house helping her streak her hair bright pink, do crazy things with makeup, draw fake tattoos on her skin using colored Sharpies and rubbing alcohol, undo the seams and hems of clothing and resew them tighter or looser or altogether differently. Often she'd want me to change the color of my hair or try a fake tattoo or alter my clothes, and I'd always laugh and say I didn't have to because I had enough fun helping her.

But the truth was that I didn't like to call attention to myself. I was happy to be the sidekick and let her have the spotlight. And that was one of the strange things about the day I met Slade — that even though I preferred to be in Jeanie's shadow, he only had eyes for me.

chapter 12

SITTING ON THE cold floor of the old EMS building, I'm worried about how my mother must be taking the news, but I'm afraid to try to get in touch with her. The police are bound to start watching, listening, tracing. Am I foolish to think I'll be safe here for the night? This was a place I'd sometimes escape to when the shouting and violent clashes at home between my brother and dad got to be too much. But that was then.

And now?

The old police scanner sits on top of the file cabinet. I push myself up and go over to it, fiddle with the knobs and switches, but the thing is lifeless. I turn away, then have a thought. Reaching behind the cabinet, I feel for the power cord and pull gently. It comes without resistance.

Easing the file cabinet out slightly, I feel along the wall for an outlet and plug the power cord in. It's only been a few weeks since the EMTs moved out, and maybe the electricity's still on. The scanner crackles loudly with static and I jump back in fright at the sudden noise. I must have accidentally turned up the volume. I quickly turn it down and look outside, as if the brief burst of sound might bring the police running.

After taking deep breaths and waiting for my heart to stop drumming, I place the scanner on the floor, where the small yellow LCD is less likely to be seen from outside. From the years of hanging around this place, I know most of the police codes and lingo and used to be able to tell—if I listened carefully enough— where every cruiser and bike cop in town was. Now voices crackle on.

Female voice: "Bravo five-eleven, what's your ten-twenty?"

Male voice: "Bravo five-eleven. Over here on Maple Hill by the house. No sign of suspect."

Female voice: "Ten-four. Bravo five-thirteen, your ten-twenty?"

Different male voice: "Bravo five-thirteen. On the Post Road, just passing Dunkin' Donuts."

Female voice: "Ten-four."

Third male voice: "Bravo five-seventeen."

Female voice: "Go ahead, Bravo five-seventeen."

Third male voice: "I've checked around the railroad station. Nothing here."

Female voice: "Ten-four, Bravo five-seventeen. Chief wants you to go over to the middle school. Look around the back."

Third male voice: "Ten-four."

The bravos are patrol cars. Maple Hill is my street. I assume Bravo 511 has been assigned to watch my house. Bravo 513 is patrolling the main street through town, the Post Road. Bravo

517 is now going to look for me behind the middle school.

None of them is anywhere near the EMS building, so that's good news for now. A yawn reaches up through me. I cover my mouth with my hand and, despite everything that's happened tonight, I'm tired enough to sleep.

Slade and his dad loved to fish and kept a boat in the harbor. Slade took me fishing a few times, but I didn't like handling the smelly chunks of bait or the slimy fish we caught. And I especially disliked the way the fish frantically flopped and squirmed before dying in a bucket.

My birthday is June 27, and the day before I turned sixteen, Slade called and told me he'd pick me up the next night and take me out to celebrate. So the next evening I put on makeup and a dress and waited. Slade showed up right on time . . . wearing old sneakers, stained jeans, and a threadbare shirt with a tear in one elbow.

"Should I change clothes?" I asked, trying to hide my disappointment.

"No, you look great," Slade said, and ushered me out to the pickup. I couldn't help noticing that in the back were fishing poles and a cooler.

"Where are we going?" I asked once I was in the pickup.

"Fishing," he answered.

We'd been dating for two years by then and I knew he was capable of playing practical jokes, so I went along with it. But when he drove to the dock and asked me to carry the poles down to the boat, I really began to wonder.

Soon we were motoring into the Sound, with the orange sun in the western sky, maybe an hour from setting. At one point Slade slowed the boat down and asked me to take the wheel, and I thought maybe then he'd do something to reveal the joke. But all he did was put two lines out to troll, and open two beers. Handing one to me, he said, "Happy birthday!" and took a big gulp.

"Are you serious?" I asked.

"Hell, yeah. It's your birthday, isn't it?" he said.

"So . . . you decided to take me fishing?"

Slade's face fell. "Don't you think it's beautiful out here?"

The water was calm and blue, and the air fresh and clear, so I said yes, it was beautiful.

"Well, I just figured maybe it was time to try fishing again," he said.

Some girls would have gotten angry, but I just felt confused. After two years, *this* was how he thought I wanted to spend my birthday? But it was a beautiful evening and we were out on the water, so I decided to make the best of it.

We traveled west for about forty-five minutes and then Slade looked at the gas gauge and said he needed to stop for fuel at a nearby marina. We pulled into a slip and started fueling and Slade went into the boat's cabin. By then the sun was close to setting and I sat in the boat, wondering how long he planned to fish.

When Slade came out of the cabin, he was wearing a jacket and tie and slacks. He offered me his arm. "Ready?"

"For what?" I asked, astonished.

"Your birthday." He pointed down the dock to a restaurant at the water's edge.

We had the best time, watching the sun go down and eating lobster. Slade had called ahead and arranged for a cake, and after dinner the waiters crowded around and sang "Happy Birthday." Knowing that blue was my favorite color, Slade gave me a sapphire ring.

Later we cruised home under the stars. Slade had one hand on the boat's wheel and his arm around me. It had gotten cooler and he'd draped his jacket over my shoulders. I was beyond happy. For the first time, I thought I knew what true love was.

chapter 13

Sunday 7:36 A.M.

IN MY DREAM *they are chasing me through the beer-kegger woods. Dakota, Mia, and the other kids, the police, the EMS squad, even Ms. Bernard, my French teacher from the fourth grade, who used to get angry when I chewed on the ends of my pens . . .*

The sound of knocking wakes me. My heart banging like a drum circle, I sit up straight and look around. It takes me a second to remember where I am. My eyes go to the window and meet Slade's. He's peeking in.

Now it comes back—why I am sleeping on this cold floor instead of in my cozy, warm bed. It's weird when you wake up from a bad dream and everything is still bad.

Tired and stiff, I get up and unlock the door. Cool, fresh air pours in as Slade enters with a brown paper bag and stares at my jeans. I look down and see why: there are ugly brownish stains on the thighs, stains we couldn't see last night in the dark.

Katherine's dried blood.

Our eyes meet. He frowns. "What happened to your face?"

I touch my face. In some places it stings. In others I feel the tiny ridges of scabs. "From running through the woods last night. I got scratched."

His forehead bunches. Is he wondering if I'm lying? "You don't think I got them from fighting with Katherine, do you?"

He shakes his head, slides into an old chair, puts down the bag, and grimaces as he massages his knee. "Chief Jenkins was on TV this morning. They want to talk to you. They're calling you a person of interest."

"What does that mean?"

He shrugs, as if he doesn't know. But I have to wonder. "You think it's a trap? Like they're hoping that if I hear I'm a person of interest and not a suspect, I'll just stroll through the front door of the police station and save them the trouble of looking for me?"

Slade scowls. "You really believe they think that way?"

"Yes." I feel my heart twist. I remember the first time I tried to tell him that I wanted to break up with him. All I could do was stare at the computer screen with tears welling up in my eyes. And Slade, sitting on his bunk bed in Georgia with his laptop, asked what was wrong and I said that nothing was wrong and I'd merely gotten something in my eyes and it was making them tear. Of course he believed me, because I'd never lied to him before.

"And if they are telling the truth and I really am just a person of interest, then it's not going to hurt if I stay away a little longer, right?"

He looks away and his mouth twists. I know him well enough to know there's something else on his mind. So I ask, "What is it?"

"Nothing." He hunches over, elbows resting on knees, his hands together, fingers knitted.

"Come on, I know you. Tell me."

Our eyes meet. He heaves a sigh. "That picture of you with the knife, kneeling next to Katherine's body? It's all over the Internet—Facebook, Twitter, everywhere. And this morning, when Chief Jenkins was on TV, they showed a photo of you from the yearbook. There's not a single person in this town who doesn't know who you are and what you look like."

It's obvious that I'm their number one suspect. That "person of interest" stuff is pure bunk.

Each May, just before Memorial Day, the PACE program put on its spring performance. Last year it was scheduled for the Friday night after Slade had left for National Guard training, and as a result, I was feeling pretty down. When Jodie, who was probably the sweetest and most thoughtful of Katherine's group, texted to ask if I needed a ride to school, I texted back that I didn't think I was going.

A few minutes later the phone rang. It was Katherine—the first time she'd ever called me. Usually she just sent texts.

"You should come," she said. "It's always fun and the cast party is a blast."

I felt my mood lift and instantly changed my mind. The mere fact that Katherine had made the effort to call and ask me to come was huge. She and Dakota were in the midst of the longest and biggest fight anyone had ever seen. Did it mean she intended to replace Dakota with me as her closest friend?

The performance was a revue, with skits and dances. Katherine and Zelda had choreographed a modern dance. Jodie did a funny monologue about a family in which everyone stole batteries from each other's TV remotes and toys.

Afterward I went backstage for the cast party. It was the first time in weeks I'd seen Katherine and Dakota in the same room, but neither spoke or even looked at the other.

It turned out that the backstage gathering wasn't the party Katherine had been talking about. The real cast party was where we all went next—at Alex Craft's house, where the punch was replaced by beer, wine coolers, and hard liquor.

Usually at parties I didn't drink more than a beer or two, but that night, because Slade had just left and I wanted to stop stressing, I let go and had a screwdriver. But the boy who mixed it made it too strong, so I went into the kitchen to add more orange juice.

I was looking in the refrigerator when I felt someone behind me. It was Dakota, holding what looked like a screwdriver in her hand. Smiling, she said, "Looking for the orange juice?"

I nodded. "Can't find any."

Dakota pressed in beside me and peered into the fridge. She pulled out a bottle of cranberry juice. "This will work."

She poured some into our glasses and we raised them. "To summer, and no more school," she toasted.

I didn't think she'd meant it maliciously, but I felt like I'd been punched in the stomach. I was dreading the end of school and the summer without Slade. Not wanting to think about that right then, I took a big gulp of my drink, even though it still tasted way too strong.

Dakota took a sip and asked, "Heard from Slade?"

I started to explain about the no-phone-calls rule and suddenly burst into tears. I'm sure it must have caught her by surprise, because I'm the last person anyone would accuse of being a drama queen. Dakota put her arms around me, and the next thing I knew, I was bawling on her shoulder.

"I'm sorry." I sniffed, embarrassed.

"No, I'm the one who should be sorry," she said. "It was a stupid thing to ask. I wasn't thinking."

When I calmed down, I went looking for a bathroom to wash my face. The downstairs bathroom was being used, so I went upstairs; only the vodka made me dizzy and I wasn't sure which door led to the bathroom. The first one I tried was a bedroom and Jodie and Zelda were inside. They were sitting on the bed with their faces close, and when I walked in, they jumped apart and both turned red, making me wonder if they'd been talking about something they didn't want me to hear.

I apologized for barging in, then found the bathroom and washed up. When I walked back out, the door to the bedroom was open and Jodie and Zelda were gone. Still feeling dizzy, I went downstairs and outside to get some fresh air. Alex's parents had white wicker furniture on the porch and I sat in a wicker love seat. The air was cool and springlike, and pretty soon things stopped spinning and I began feel better. Then the front door opened and Katherine came out. "Want some company?" she asked, sounding sweet and concerned.

"Sure."

She sat down beside me in the love seat. "How are you feeling?"

"A little better, thanks," I said.

Katherine moved close and put her arm around my shoulders. She'd never done anything like that before. "You really love him."

"I think so."

"You just *think* so?" she asked.

"No, no, I mean yes, I really do."

"It's amazing, you know?" Katherine said.

"What is?"

"Just that you can be so sure. I mean, like, at our age. And you are sure, aren't you?"

It was strange how she always seemed to know what was on my mind. "I don't know," I admitted. "I mean, yes, I'm sure I love him, but I'm not sure what I'll do if he gets sent overseas for a long time. I won't be seventeen until almost July. It feels too young to have to wait so long."

"I can imagine."

I turned and looked at her. "You can? Really?"

Katherine nodded sympathetically and hooked her light brown hair behind her ear. She was wearing ear knots with little green whales. "Sure. Like you said, we're sixteen. How can we really know what we want?"

I looked into her eyes, which that night were unexpectedly kind and caring. "Can I tell you a secret?"

She nodded.

"Sometimes I feel like I need Slade more than I want him. Like we've been together for so long that I'm afraid of what life would be like without him."

Katherine squeezed my shoulder. "I think you'd be fine."

The front door opened and Dakota came out. When she saw Katherine and me, she stopped and stared, then spun around and went back inside, slamming the door so hard behind her I thought the glass might break. Beside me, Katherine sighed loudly, then said, "Sorry, I have to go."

Sunday 4:37 P.M.

I KNOW THE yearbook photo Slade was talking about. In it I've got shoulder-length blonde hair and a bright smile. A lot of that hair is now at the bottom of a brown paper bag, and what's left on my head is jet-black and spiky. I'm wearing enough black eye makeup to pass for a raccoon, and I dyed and plucked my eyebrows until they were thin black slivers to go with my black lips and nails. Topping it all off is a thick, abstract Sharpie tattoo on the side of my neck. Thanks to the rubbing alcohol, it looks almost real.

The police scanner blurts on.

Female voice: "Bravo five-eleven, what's your ten-twenty?"

Male voice: "Bravo five-eleven. Over by the train station."

Female voice: "Go over to Kearn's Deli. Ten-sixty-two on a possible sighting of person wanted for questioning."

Male voice: "Ten-four."

A 10-62 means to take a report from a citizen. I don't think it's paranoid to imagine that the person wanted for questioning is me. So that means someone thinks he or she saw me and has called the police to report it. Of course, it's a mistake. No one's seen me. No one . . . except Slade.

I feel my stomach knot, from both hunger and anxiety, and I rip out the seams of Alyssa's jeans and resew them so they're skinny, then rip the knees and a pocket before scrawling on them and the sneakers with black Sharpies. All this work keeps me busy until, despite my nervousness, I'm starving. Finally, stomach grumbling, I stand before the bathroom mirror and consider what I've created. Scratches hidden by makeup. Black hair, black eyes and lips, black clothes. Short of piercings, I am as punk as can be.

But now I have to leave this place, and if this disguise doesn't work, I won't be punk. I'll be in jail.

If, as I suspected, Dakota was Katherine's killer, I wouldn't be totally surprised. I had learned that she was practiced at appearing to be things she wasn't. I knew, for instance, that she could be fast and aggressive with boys, even if she pretended to be the opposite. Even though she was pretty, with shoulder-length auburn hair, a trim figure, and an unusually ample chest for a girl her size, she never talked about dating. And while lots of girls wore tight low-cut tops and flaunted their cleavage, she stuck to turtlenecks and blouses.

But Slade had told me what had happened while he and his dad had been doing the renovation of the Jenkinses' kitchen. Dakota had taken a shine to one of the workers, a guy about Slade's age. She started hanging around, finding excuses to talk to him, "accidentally" bumping into him, and dropping hints.

"What kind of hints?" I asked.

"Oh, you know." Slade reddened slightly. "The kind of stuff a girl does and says when she's interested. And she'd touch him, too, when she talked."

"Your friend told you that?"

"Yeah. I mean, it was kind of weird. Not the kind of thing that happens a lot when you're on a job."

"What did he do?"

"Well, that's where it got even weirder, because there's this unwritten rule that you don't mix business with pleasure, *especially* when it's the daughter of the client. So at first the guy just tried to laugh it off, but the more he did that, the more insistent she got. Like once she set her mind on something, she had to have it. Finally the foreman had to take him off that job and put him on another one." He paused for a second, then added, "But even that wasn't the end of it. She got hold of his phone number and sent some text messages. You know, that kind of thing."

"So . . . she was really aggressive?"

Slade nodded. It sounded strange. Not that a girl would do something like that but that the girl in question was Dakota.

"And?"

"Don't really know. After that, I never heard anything more about it."

chapter 15

Sunday 4:42 P.M.

IN THE OLD EMS building, my hand trembles as I reach for the door. Who would imagine that going outside could be this hard? But I'm scared. What will happen if I get caught? Who'll defend me? My mother has no money. She used everything she had on Sebastian's defense and then had to declare bankruptcy. And despite all that, Sebastian is still in jail with an eight-to-fifteen-year sentence for aggravated assault. It would have been worse had it not been for the private defense lawyer paid for by his friend Jerry.

But I can't hide forever, so out I go. It's early September and everything is still green and warm. I walk along the sidewalk toward town, looking straight ahead and taking determined steps. I remember something Jodie once said: *A costume is the least convincing part of a role. It's the acting that makes or breaks you.* My only chance is to act like I'm just another punk with some-place to go.

It's a good thing no one can hear the thudding of my heart.

First stop is the convenience store. As I walk in, my eyes go immediately to the newspaper stand by the door. On the front page of the local paper is a large slightly blurred color photo that I try not to focus on, knowing it must be one of the shots of me kneeling beside Katherine's body. Above it in big thick black letters is the headline.

POLICE SEARCH FOR LOCAL TEEN IN MURDER INVESTIGATION

Sex Assault Considered Possible Motive

Sex assault? I want to pick up the paper and read it, but I can't. *Don't look*, I tell myself. *Act normal.* There are a few other customers in the store, but I don't look at them, either. As I pull a prepackaged ham-and-cheese sandwich out of the refrigerated display and grab a soda, I consider what this unexpected development could mean. If it was a sex assault, then it couldn't have been Dakota. But then who killed Katherine? Is it possible Slade was right? That it was just some random stranger?

But if they think it was a sex assault, why are they looking for me?

I head for the checkout, but as I'm paying, I notice the black-and-white monitor in the corner, where the walls meet the ceiling. And there I am on the screen with my new black spiky hair. I quickly look away, but not before a cold chill envelops me. I don't know why the sight of me on the security monitor should freak me out more than the photo on the front of the newspaper, but it does. It's like the picture in the newspaper was then and the monitor is now, so they have a record of me in disguise on video. Suddenly I just want to get out of there as fast as my feet can take me.

Back on the sidewalk, I have one more stop to make—the hardware store—but walking through town is nerve-racking. Every time I pass a person, every time someone glances in my direction, I wonder if he or she can see through my disguise. With every step, I have to fight the urge to bolt.

Inside the hardware store, I select some small brass-colored key rings and take them up to the register, once again aware of the video camera mounted in the corner. I'm so busy trying to position myself so that the camera doesn't see my face that I don't focus on the person at the cash register until it's my turn to pay.

We're practically eye to eye. *Oh my God!* She's a punk with hot pink streaks in her dirty blonde hair and tattoos and piercings. We stare at each other for a moment. Soundview isn't exactly a mecca for punks. Is she wondering why she's never seen me around before? Does she know why I'm buying those small key rings? She calculates the price and I feverishly dig into my pockets for the money. The change slips through my shaking fingers and clatters on the counter.

"Oh, sorry!" I blurt.

She cocks her head curiously and stares as she picks up the coins she needs. "New around here?"

"Uh . . ." I slide the rest of the change into my shaking hand, trying to think of an answer. "No. I mean, yes!"

She frowns. Terrified that I've blown it, I shove the change into my pocket and turn to go. I'm just pushing through the door when she calls, "Hey, stop!"

Katherine might have been right about one thing: maybe three years is a long time to date someone. I was almost always happy with Slade, but that doesn't mean it was always easy. Sometimes he grew glum, withdrawn, and depressed; a few times it was so deep that it scared me. A couple of times I suggested he speak to Dr. Ploumis, the school psychologist, or find a psychologist outside school to speak to, but he always said he'd think about it, which was his way of saying no.

Once when I pressed him about why he wouldn't seek help, he said his father wouldn't understand. I said that was silly. This was the twenty-first century. Everyone understood that sometimes you needed help and that was what psychologists were for. Look at how many kids we knew who were on some kind of medication. But Slade would insist that his father was too old-school for that. You manned up and toughed it out. Shrinks were for wimps and the only medication a man needed came in an amber bottle with a black-and-white label.

One night last spring, just before Slade went away for National Guard training, he got really, really low. A bunch of us were at Dog Beach, a small strip of rock and sand squeezed between two fancy beach clubs. It was a place where people could look for sea glass or bring their dogs for a swim. At one end of the beach, a long, tall metal pier stretched into the Sound. The pier was high enough that sometimes guys would climb through the metal crosshatched supports until they were over the water, and smoke or drink out there just for a change of view.

On this night I'd been talking to some girls when I realized I hadn't seen Slade for a while. It wasn't like him to vanish without telling me, and I began to feel anxious. I looked around and noticed the silhouette of a figure perched in the crosshatching under the pier. I knew at once that it had to be Slade, but I couldn't imagine what he was doing out there. I thought of walking to the water's edge and calling to him, but something told me he didn't want everyone's attention.

Instead, I climbed up into the supports and started to make my way under the pier. It wasn't easy. The way the supports were staggered, you needed pretty long arms to get from one to the next, and being under five feet tall, I had to take a few leaps of faith. But I didn't think twice. Going all the way out there by himself was unlike Slade. I knew something was wrong.

He heard me when I was about a dozen feet away. I saw his head turn and knew he was looking, even though in the dark under the pier, I couldn't see his face. I paused, planting my feet in the **V** of the supports, and waited for him to say something.

It was a while before he said, "What are you doing here, Shrimp?"

"What are *you* doing here?" I replied.

He looked away, at the water. It was a cloudy, dark night with only a pale outline of a quarter moon appearing from and disappearing behind the clouds. I climbed closer, but the way the supports were set up, there wasn't room for me to sit beside him. I had to stop about three feet away. Just out of reach.

"Slade?" I said softly. "What is it?"

"I don't want to go," he said without looking at me, his voice breathy, almost breaking. He was talking about the National Guard.

"Let's go back to the beach," I said.

He didn't react.

"Slade?"

"Why do I have to do all these things just because my father wants me to? You know they're sending Guard units overseas? Every week guardsmen are getting killed? And for what?"

"Maybe you won't get sent."

"Oh, great. And then I get to look forward to spending the rest of my life working in drywall. Whoop-de-do!"

I was surprised to hear him put into words what I'd sensed he'd been feeling for a long time. "You don't have to."

I heard him exhale slowly, and then he tilted his head down. "It'll kill him. I mean, first my mom. Then that stupid second marriage. Then my brother moving to Boston and my sister moving to Florida. And what about Alyssa?"

Slade's mom had died of breast cancer when he was five. A failed second marriage had left Mr. Lamont with joint custody of Alyssa. Since then, Mr. Lamont had resigned himself to single fatherhood, and many lonely nights in front of the TV in the company of a bottle of Jack Daniel's. Sometimes it worried me that Slade seemed to be following in his father's footsteps. The solitary drinking and solemn, silent moods during which he didn't want to go anywhere or do anything.

"It's your life, Slade," I said. "If you don't want to work with him—"

"Might as well," he muttered, cutting me off. "Don't know what else to do . . . unless it's to just end it all."

"Slade!" I hated when he talked like that. "Please, let's go back."

But he didn't answer. Below us, small waves splashed against the rocks and pilings. I knew he was upset about leaving me, because that was how I was feeling about seeing him go. The longest we'd ever been apart was maybe four or five days.

"I love you," I said. "We'll talk every day, I promise."

He looked away into the dark. "I have news for you, Cal. We *won't* talk every day. I read the regulations. For the first two months of basic training, you're allowed just one phone call—to your parents."

That took me by surprise. "Two months isn't that long. You won't believe how fast it'll go." It was strange. He'd just turned nineteen and I was still a month from turning seventeen, yet there were times when I felt like I had to fill in for his mother. In my own dark moments, I sometimes wondered if it would always be this way. Would I have to struggle to get him out of these moods for the rest of my life?

Under the pier Slade turned to me again and for a second I thought his eyes were glistening, but then a cloud covered the moon and it was too dark to be sure. "You promise?" he asked.

"Yes, all of it. I promise I'll always love you, and after those first two months, we'll talk every day and it'll go fast. Now come on, let's go back to the beach."

Slade nodded and reached up toward something. It was only then that I noticed the belt. It was hanging from one of the supports as if it had been tied there. At the other end the belt looped over on itself through the buckle. I didn't know if Slade meant it seriously or just as a symbol, but it looked like a noose.

chapter 16

Sunday 4:54 P.M.

WHEN I HEAR the punk cashier in the hardware store yell, "Hey, stop!" my first inclination is to bolt through the door and down the sidewalk as fast as I can. It would be the natural, logical thing to do in my situation, right? So I don't know where the guile and wherewithal that keeps me from running comes from. Maybe I just know that once I start to run, I'm bound to be caught. So somehow, even though my heart is racing and I feel like I want to jump out of my skin, I force myself to stop and turn to look at her.

She's holding out a small brown paper bag. "You forgot this."

I force a smile and take the bag. "Thanks."

And then I'm out of there.

At the bus stop, despite my hunger, I'm too wound up to eat the sandwich I bought. So I sit and stare down at my black fingernails. Thank God the bus comes soon and it's almost empty. Sitting near the back, I wolf down the sandwich and wish I'd bought a second one. Then I get to work on the key rings, snipping them with the wire cutters to leave just enough of a gap to squeeze some flesh into. One goes on my lip, two on a nostril, one on an eyebrow, and the rest on my ears. Jeanie once told me something funny about piercings: When you have them, people don't focus on you. They focus on the hardware.

I got on the bus with no piercings. Thirty-five minutes later, at the stop by Fairchester Community College, I get off in full metallic regalia.

I've come to FCC to find Tallon Marx, who is studying for a degree in math with a minor in physical education. Last year she was a teaching assistant at Soundview High, helped coach the girls' cross-country team, and worked in PACE. Because she was cool and smart and only a few years older than us, she became a confidant and a go-to person when someone had a problem or needed the kind of advice she didn't feel comfortable going to a friend or an adult for.

At a house that has been divided into units, I ring Tallon's bell and wait, praying she's there. A lock clacks and the door opens a few inches, but it's not Tallon; it's her roommate, Jasmine, who has freckles and spidery red dreadlocks. "Yes?"

A cold shiver runs through me. She's staring right at me, at my fake piercings and spiked dyed hair. If she's watched TV or been on the computer, will she recognize me? But there's more confusion than recognition in her eyes.

"Hi," I say. "You're Jasmine, right? Is Tallon around?"

Jasmine frowns, as if she can't quite figure out how I know her name and why someone who looks like me would be asking for Tallon. But the good news is that she's treating me like a stranger, not like a suspect in a murder. "She went to the library, but she should be back soon. Is . . . there something I can help you with?"

"I—" I almost say that I'm a friend of Tallon's from Soundview High, but I catch myself. What if Tallon's told her about the girl she knew from last year who the police are looking for in connection with a murder? "I'm here for tutoring? In math? Tallon said if she wasn't here, you could let me in."

Jasmine scowls but opens the door a little bit wider. "She didn't say anything about tutoring."

"Oh, yeah, she put a sign up in my school."

Jasmine bites a corner of her lip, obviously still uncertain about what to do.

"I can wait out here in the hall if you'd like," I offer with less-than-complete sincerity. I'd much rather wait inside, where there's less chance of being spotted.

The ploy works. "Oh, no, you can come in," she says.

I go in, glad to get out of the hall. Jasmine gestures to a couch covered by an Indian-print spread. The couch creaks and feels lumpy. To my right is a tiny standing-room-only kitchen.

"Can I get you something to drink?" Jasmine asks.

"I'm fine, thanks."

She twirls a dreadlock around with her finger and gestures to a door with an art poster on it. "Well, uh, I have to study. I'm sure Tallon will be here any time now."

"Thanks." I give her a wave.

Even in the apartment I feel nervous. What if Jasmine did recognize me and just pretended not to? What if the next person through the door isn't Tallon but a police officer? Being tense and alert all the time is draining, and that is coupled with the little sleep I got last night. My senses are dulled and sketchy, as if I could easily miss something important because my brain can't process as quickly or as thoroughly as normal. I try to practice what I'll say to Tallon but I'm so woozy and sleep-deprived that it's difficult to put words together.

The door opens and Tallon comes in, carrying a green backpack with a peace symbol on it. Her dark hair is longer than it was last year and she's wearing lots of silver bangles and rings. She sees me on the couch and gives me an uncertain smile. "Hi."

"Hi, Tallon."

She cocks her head and furrows her brow, as if she's trying to figure out what her connection to this small punk girl could be. I stand up and the perplexed look on her face gradually morphs into one of astonishment.

"Callie?" she gasps.

I press a finger to my lips. "I have to talk to you."

Tallon's eyes dart left and right, as if she's wondering what to do now that she's discovered a killer in her apartment.

The door with the art poster opens and Jasmine sticks her head out. "Tallon, can I speak to you for a second?"

Tallon's head swings back and forth between her roommate and me. My insides clench. They know something's wrong. I have to get out of here.

"You know she hates her," Jodie once said. We were sitting in Dakota's backyard, watching her play Katherine in badminton.

"But they're best friends," I said.

"You know what the Chinese general said? 'Keep your friends close, and your enemies closer.'"

I thought about it, but didn't see how it related to Dakota and Katherine. "What makes you say that?"

"Watch."

I watched. To me they looked like two red-faced girls careening and swinging and trying to win a silly game that involved hitting a strange little bally thing over a high net. Katherine, with her compact, boyish body, was a model of deft movement and quick reflexes. Dakota, with her heavy, bouncing chest, often appeared off balance and seemed to lurch from one shot to the next. Neither girl smiled, whereas I imagined that I would have had a hard time not laughing at the absurdity of it. But if there was one thing Dakota and Katherine had in common, it was how serious and determined they were about almost everything.

"They just look like they always do to me," I said.

Jodie turned and studied me for a moment, as if searching for some clue to why I couldn't see what she saw. Then she lowered her voice and said, "You can't see that Dakota is one inch from smashing her racket into Katherine's face?"

"Ahhh!" Just then Dakota yelped in frustration as the shuttlecock fell to the ground on her side. On the other side of the net, Katherine grinned triumphantly, red-faced and panting, with her hands on her hips.

"I hate you!" Dakota cried, picking up the shuttlecock.

"No, you don't," Katherine said.

"Oh, I *so* hate you!" Dakota insisted, and served. Once again they started batting the little ball back and forth. And almost immediately Katherine hit it just out of Dakota's reach.

"Grrrrr." Her face glistening, Dakota gritted her teeth and kept playing.

"Did Dakota say something?" I whispered to Jodie.

"No. She never talks about Katherine. Ever. Even that's a sign. It's like she knows she can't trust herself to say the right thing. I mean, think about the family she comes from. They're all politicians. It's all about saying and doing the right thing."

That might have been true, but it also meant that Jodie had no real evidence of animosity between the two girls. Meanwhile, Dakota and Katherine were once again absorbed in thrashing at the shuttlecock. Still whispering, I asked, "I know what you said about the Chinese general, but seriously, if Dakota hates Katherine so much, why does she want to be her friend?"

"Because they both want the same thing."

Before I could ask what that thing was, Katherine balled her hand into a fist and cried, "Yes!"

On the other side of the net, Dakota took several determined steps toward a large potted plant nearby and swung the racket down as hard as she could. *Crack!* I jumped at the sound of the frame shattering against the edge of the clay pot. Dakota tossed the broken racket away and purposefully stood with her back toward us, as if she didn't want us to see how furious she was.

Katherine smiled, as if she enjoyed causing so much anguish. "I'm getting something to drink," she announced, dropping her racket in the grass, wiping her forehead with the back of her hand, and heading toward the house.

Dakota stood by the badminton net—her face red and glistening, her eyes narrowed, her jaw clenched—glowering as if she were ready to kill. I felt an elbow touch my arm and turned to find Jodie with one eyebrow raised as if to say, *See?*

chapter 17

Sunday 5:08 P.M.

THE FRONT DOOR of the apartment is across the room. I'll have to get past Tallon to reach it.

Once again Jasmine says insistently, "Tallon?"

"Can it wait?" Tallon answers, clearly uncomfortable about taking her eyes off me.

I decide to take a step, to see how she reacts.

"I'd appreciate it next time if you'd ask before you use our living room for tutoring," Jasmine says in a huff, and closes her door.

Tallon turns and stares at me, clearly bewildered.

"For God's sake, Tallon," I whisper, "do you really think I could kill anyone?"

"But the pictures . . ."

I start to whisper fast, desperate to make her understand before she screams for help. "She was dead when I found her, and someone took a picture that made it look like I did it." I just hope Jasmine doesn't have her ear pressed to the door. "Can't we talk someplace more private?"

Tallon stiffens. Does she think that maybe this is my way of getting her alone so that I can stab her, too? Callie Carson, serial maniac killer. Tallon has definitely been watching too much *CSI*. I pat my pockets and turn my palms out, showing her that I'm not carrying any weapons. "Tallon, please. This is *serious*. I'm desperate. You have to listen."

She gestures to the couch and takes a seat on the other side of the small coffee table. "If you didn't do it, why not just go to the police and tell them what happened?"

"You saw the pictures. Everyone thinks I did it. I mean, come on, you think I did it, too."

Tallon averts her eyes, more or less confirming what I've just said. "There was something on the news this morning about how it might have been sexual," she says in a low voice. "If that's the case, why would they be looking for you?"

"I don't know," I said. "There are a lot of things about this that don't make sense."

Tallon studies me. "Why *did* you come here?"

"Last spring, a few weeks before the PACE show, something happened between Dakota and Katherine. Like, for a couple of weeks they were completely icy to each other. Didn't speak, wouldn't even look at each other. Dakota wouldn't even come into the cafeteria at lunch. I know they fought a lot, but this time it was different. It went on for much longer and seemed more serious. And then it went back to normal. I came here to see if you know what happened."

Tallon's eyebrows rise. I was worried that she wouldn't even know what I was talking about, but her reaction tells me she knows *exactly*. "Why do you want to know about that?"

I have to answer carefully. I don't want her to think that I may be trying to pin Katherine's murder on Dakota. "I . . . heard something."

The faint lines around Tallon's eyes deepen and she slowly nods her head. "It was really personal, Callie. I can't imagine how it could have had anything to do with Katherine getting killed. It would be pretty far-fetched, don't you think?"

I have no idea what she's talking about, but I have to pretend. "It may be far-fetched, but put yourself in my place. Right now it's all I've got to go on. It may be a dead end, or maybe it will lead to something else."

Tallon purses her lips, as if she's not sure what to do. I wonder why she doesn't just tell me to go ask Dakota about it, but clearly something is making her hesitate. "Listen, Callie, I understand that this is incredibly serious for you, but the reason people confide in me is because they trust me. I can't go revealing the intimate details of someone's life just because you think there's a slim chance it might pertain to your situation. I'm really sorry, but frankly, I can't see how these two things could be connected. I mean, we both know what you're implying. Do you really think Dakota is capable of doing something like that?"

It's hard for me not to jump up and gasp, *Yes!* But I can't, because I have no idea what Tallon's talking about. What intimate details?

"I know," I reply, trying to sound like I'm commiserating about the situation she's in. "You don't want to betray anyone's trust. It's just . . . they ran so hot and cold."

"What do you expect? They're rivals. If it wasn't for Katherine, Dakota would be the queen."

If I can just keep her talking . . . "But what happened before the PACE show felt different. More serious."

Tallon lets out a sigh, as if she's torn about what to do. "Well, I guess the only other person you could speak to would be Griffen himself."

Griffen?

The bedroom door opens and Jasmine comes out. She looks at us and frowns. If Tallon's tutoring me, why aren't there books open on the coffee table? I've raised her suspicions and put Tallon in an awkward situation. And who is this Griffen person?

Jasmine goes into the kitchen and I hear water running. Tallon leans close to me and whispers, "You have to go. You know the police want anyone who sees you to report it. I could get into really big trouble for this."

I slowly start to rise and whisper, "I would have gone to Griffen in the first place, but I didn't know how to find him."

"I'm sure he's on Facebook," Tallon whispers back.

We start to cross the living room. I can feel Jasmine's eyes on me. We get to the door, but instead of going through it, I hesitate and say, "I would have tried Facebook, but I forgot his last name."

"Clemment," Tallon whispers urgently, as if she wants me to leave, now!

"Right. Thanks." I go out the door and down the steps as fast as I can without appearing to run.

By the time I reach the sidewalk, I've already decided that I can't go back to the bus stop. If Tallon calls the police, I'll be too easy to spot there. Besides, I have to get to a computer. FCC has a library, so I head toward campus. Fortunately it's Sunday and not many people are around.

I find the library. At a computer inside I settle down, sign into Facebook, and search Griffen Clemment. A page comes up with a photo of a guy with longish straight blond hair. He's wearing a white oxford shirt and plaid shorts and standing on the deck of a sailboat, looking as if he's posing in an ad. The message beside the picture states, *Griffen Clemment only shares some of his profile information with everyone. If you know Griffen, send him a message or add him as a friend.*

Under *Groups* it states *Meadows School.*

Bingo! That's a private school nearby.

Suddenly a chat box opens on the screen and I am staring at a photo of Mia. In the chat box she types, **Callie?**

I freeze, realizing I've just made a mistake. Now that I've signed on, every Facebook friend I have who is also online right now knows it.

Mia: **Is this U? OMG! WRU?**

Cal: **Not imprtnt.**

Mia: **The police R looking 4 U.**

Cal: **I no.**

Mia: **Why R U hiding?**

Cal: **Didnt do it.**

Mia: **We have 2 meet f2f.**

Before I can answer, the screen starts to populate with chat boxes from other kids I know. The news that Callie Carson is online is spreading fast. I have to get off.

I hate the way people toss around the phrase "dysfunctional family" and make jokes out of it. I remember one about someone putting the "fun" in "dysfunctional." I don't mean to be a downer but it's not funny. Not if you really live in one.

When Dad and Sebastian went at it, Mom couldn't, or wouldn't, leave. Maybe she believed that if she stayed, it would stop things from really getting out of control. Or maybe it was to be around in case someone got hurt and needed care. Or maybe it was simply that this was her family and she was part of it.

Everyone who knew us knew that it was slowly destroying her. Even before the night Sebastian assaulted Dad with the two-by-four, Mom had begun to come apart. There were days when she couldn't get out of bed and days when she could only sit, zombielike, in front of the TV. The house became filthy. Meals weren't prepared.

In a bizarre way, the last fight between Sebastian and Dad was both the end and the beginning. It was the end of the war in our family, and the end of Mom's hopes. But it was the beginning of her new role as caretaker. It gave her a purpose and a reason to get out of bed in the morning, even if caring for her husband was, in its own way, a prison sentence.

chapter 18

IN THE FCC library I quickly sign off Facebook and stare at the dark computer screen. Can they trace my log-in back to this computer? I doubt it. But just to be safe, I'd better get out of here.

Why did Mia write that she had to meet me face-to-face?

Outside, it's getting dark. I head back to the bus stop, but as I round a corner, I see a plain gray sedan with two people inside parked beside the sidewalk. I freeze, then quickly back around the corner of a building. I've seen enough unmarked police cars to know. A wretched thought: Did Tallon call them?

I double back the way I came and walk half a dozen blocks to the next bus stop, then watch carefully from across the street until I see the bus coming. At the last moment I dash across the street and board it.

By the time I get back to Soundview, it's dark. But before I head to the EMS building, there's one more stop I must make. Umbrella Point is a rock outcropping at the end of the small park that runs along the water in the part of town known as the Manor. Mounted in the rocks is an umbrella made of wood and shingles. On almost every precipitation-free day when the temperature reaches forty-five and there aren't gale-force winds, Mom takes Dad down there in his wheelchair to sit by the water and watch the boats.

Last night, when I spoke to Mom on the phone, I told her to look under the umbrella. Now, in one of the wooden crevices, I leave a note reassuring her that I'm okay, promising that I'll leave more notes, and pleading with her not to tell anyone.

It's late by the time I let myself back into the old EMS building. I'm really not looking forward to another night alone in here. And knowing the name of the boy who may have caused that huge rift between Katherine and Dakota isn't enough to make me feel encouraged. But it's all I've got.

Sitting on the cold floor of the dark, abandoned building, I flip open my phone and turn it on. It registers nearly two dozen missed calls, mostly from my mother and Mia, but I'll run down the battery if I listen to the messages. Instead, I call Slade, who answers almost immediately.

"Hey." He sounds solemn. I wish he'd be more excited and happy to hear from me. But I know better than to think that in one night I could undo all the damage I caused. Two steps forward, one step back.

Even though I'm feeling discouraged, I'm eager to tell him what I learned about Griffen Clemment. "Listen, I found out something—"

"Hold on, Cal." He cuts me short. "There's something you

need to know. Dakota's mother was on TV just now, talking about what a horrible tragedy it is that Katherine was killed and how devastated Dakota is."

That strikes me as strange. Why would Congresswoman Jenkins get involved? Could it be that she knows the truth about her daughter and is trying to steer the investigation away from her?

Slade continues: "They showed that photo of you again. The one with you kneeling over her with the knife in your—"

He's still talking, but I'm no longer focused on what he's saying. The scanner has stopped scanning and is locked on one frequency. "Ten-twenty-nine," a female voice says urgently. "The old EMS building on Palmer. All patrol vehicles in the vicinity. Code two. Repeat. All vehicles. Ten-twenty-nine. Code two. The old EMS building on Palmer."

"Bravo five-eleven. Got it, ten-four," a male voice replies.

"Bravo five-sixteen. Ten-four," radios another male voice.

Ten-twenty-nine probably means "suspect wanted." Code two is when they want the police to approach without lights or sirens. They're coming here.

Right now.

Zelda's house was closer to a mansion than anything else in town. It was a huge old three-story brick colonial with a pool and a tennis court. One afternoon last July, Katherine and Dakota were sunning themselves on the lounges, and Zelda and I were in the pool, floating on inflatable rafts with beverage holders and shades so you could keep your face from getting too much sun.

"Want to have a contest?" Zelda asked. "Who can hold her breath longer?"

"Okay," I said.

We slid off the rafts and into the cool clear water. Zelda turned to Dakota. "Time us?"

Dakota reached for her phone and flipped it open. "Uh . . . ready, set, go!"

Zelda and I both ducked under the surface. Unlike the town pool's, this water didn't burn your eyes. We stayed down, holding the chrome bars to keep from floating up, our lips pressed together and our hair swirling around us. I could feel my heart thumping and my lungs beginning to hurt. At almost the same moment, Zelda and I let some air out of our mouths and grinned at each other as the silver bubbles raced to the surface.

My lungs began to burn. I imaged Zelda's did, too. I fought the urge to let go and shoot to the surface. If Zelda could stay down that long, so could I. But the discomfort continued to increase, until finally I had to pull myself to the surface for air.

"A minute and twelve seconds," Dakota announced. Meanwhile, in the lounge beside her, Katherine had her phone pressed to her ear.

And Zelda was still beneath the surface.

"A minute and twenty seconds," Dakota said.

Ten seconds later, she said, "Thirty."

"Hold on," Katherine said to whomever she was speaking to. She leaned forward curiously on her lounge to look down at Zelda.

"A minute forty," Dakota announced.

Several seconds later, Zelda splashed to the surface.

"A minute and forty-seven seconds," Dakota said.

Zelda grinned triumphantly.

"That's amazing," I said.

"My dad and I have contests all the time," Zelda said breathlessly, her wet hair plastered to her head. "I always beat him, too."

"I'll call you back," Katherine said into her phone, and snapped it shut.

"What's the longest you've stayed under?"

"A little over two minutes," Zelda answered.

Katherine pointed at her phone. "Know who that was? Mia. She wanted to know what we were doing."

"What did you tell her?" Dakota asked.

Katherine smiled and flipped open the phone. "I think I'm going to invite her over."

Sunday 8:32 P.M.

IN THE EMS building the seconds are ticking past. *Get out of here!* I tell myself, then go through the door and dash away into the dark. As I head into the woods beyond the parking lot, my first thought is to run as far and as fast as I can, but maybe that's a mistake. Maybe I should crouch down behind a tree and wait and watch.

There's just enough moonlight for me to make out the two police cruisers that roll quietly into the parking lot with their lights off. A police officer from each unit gets out, and they silently gesture to each other in the dark. One goes around behind the building, as if to catch anyone who may try to escape out the back. The other tiptoes quietly toward the front door. In the dark I can tell that each is carrying things in his hands, but I can't tell what. Flashlights?

Guns?

The thought sends a shiver through me. How can it be that the police believe I'm so dangerous that they need to have their weapons out? It seems unreal. I'm just a teenager . . . and a girl, for God's sake. But they think I'm a killer. And if I've killed once, there's nothing to stop me from killing again, right?

One of the police officers is at the door now. His flashlight goes on and he looks through the window as he reaches for the doorknob. The door doesn't open. I must have locked it accidentally when I ran out. He goes back to the cruiser, opens the trunk, and returns with a crowbar.

But before he gets back to the door, the whole scene is suddenly illuminated by headlights. It's another car. The officer with the crowbar shields his eyes from the glare as the car stops and someone jumps out. I can't tell for certain, but I think it's a woman.

"You are interfering with an ongoing police investigation!" the officer announces loudly. "Get out of here! Now!"

The woman hesitates and takes a step back toward her car, but now another car pulls in. The officer with the crowbar curses as a person gets out of the second car and raises something to his face. A flash goes off.

The police officer repeats what he told the woman. "You're interfering with a police investigation!" By now I've realized what's happening. I'm not the only person who's been listening to a police scanner. News reporters have them, too.

As if the officer with the crowbar has just realized the same thing, he turns back to the building and begins prying open the door before more unwanted visitors arrive. The photographer quickly moves in, snapping flash after flash.

For a moment I can't help feeling amazed that they're doing all this on my account. Then I remember that it's not about me; it's about Katherine. The door pops open and the officer enters. The lights go on, and from my spot in the woods, I can see the dark silhouette of the officer cautiously moving around inside as if he's looking for me.

He disappears from view, then returns a little bit later. Even from a distance I can tell by his movements that he's more relaxed now, as if he knows that the place is empty. The other officer joins him. One of them picks up something brown, and when they shine a flashlight into it, I realize it's the paper bag with my hair. Next one of them holds up something darker. I have a feeling they're my bloodstained jeans. Now both officers leave the EMS building. While one puts the bag and the jeans into his cruiser, the other sweeps his flashlight across the woods. Now the first one joins him. Together they swing their flashlights around, illuminating tree trunks and brush.

They separate and move toward the trees, flashlights bright.

And one of them is coming straight toward me.

Katherine told Zelda to stay in the pool while the rest of us went into the kitchen. The plan called for Dakota to stay near the window. When Dakota tugged on her right earlobe, Zelda was to float facedown in the pool as if she'd drowned.

We were eating chips and fruit when Mia arrived, breathless and obviously thrilled to be invited. She looked around Zelda's kitchen with wide eyes and I realized that, like me, she was here for the first time. "Where's Zelda?"

"Oh, still out in the pool, I guess," Katherine replied nonchalantly, and gestured toward the door. "Go out and say hi."

As Mia crossed the kitchen, Dakota, standing by the window, tugged her earlobe. I felt my heart start to thud. I really didn't want to be part of something so cruel. I wanted to tell Mia that she should stop, that it was a trick. But I didn't. We watched her go out to the pool. All we could see was her back. Halfway there she stopped. Her shoulders rose and tightened. She rushed forward and stopped at the edge. Her hands rose to shoulder height, her fingers spread. I couldn't see her face, but I imagined her yelling. Her head swiveled as she looked back toward the kitchen, clearly gripped with panic, her eyes wide, her mouth agape.

Standing at the kitchen counter, Katherine was smiling, her eyes shining with delight.

Meanwhile, Mia twisted back and forth between the pool and the kitchen as if she couldn't decide what to do. Her body movements and the expression on her face were frantic.

"Pretend nothing's wrong," Katherine hissed, and looked down at a magazine on the kitchen counter. Across the kitchen Dakota turned away from the window.

Mia burst through the kitchen door and cried, "Something's wrong! I think maybe Zelda's drowned! Call 911!"

Katherine calmly lifted her face from the magazine and scowled. "What makes you think that?"

"She's floating facedown in the pool!" Mia cried. "Call 911. Oh my God, we have to do something!"

"It's a trick," I said, no longer able to restrain myself. I pointed at the pool, where Zelda raised her head as if to see what was happening. Mia's mouth fell open.

Katherine shot me an icy look. Then, with a grin, she turned to Mia and laughed. "Fooled you!"

Mia's red face at first reflected her confusion, and then, blinking hard, she forced a smile onto her lips. "A joke? It was a joke?"

She managed one frail laugh . . . then disintegrated into tears and ran out of the kitchen.

There was silence. Once again Katherine's expression turned cold as she glared at me. "You ruined it."

chapter 20

Sunday 8:46 P.M.

AS THE POLICE officer with the flashlight approaches the woods, the beam burns circles in my eyes. The tree I'm crouched behind isn't big enough to hide me. I have to make a decision: run or hide? Running means making noise and being easy to spot. Hiding means I'm a sitting duck if he finds me. Now I curse myself for not running sooner. Why did I stay and watch?

My inclination is to run. It's what I've always done. But something inside tells me not to. If I run now, it'll be in the dark, through woods, while I'm chased by a man with a flashlight and with a radio to call in backup.

Instead, I peer around in the dark, searching for a better hiding place.

Meanwhile, the flashlight beam is getting brighter.

There's a cluster of bushes to my right. But if I were searching for someone, wouldn't that be where I'd look?

To my left is a big tree with a wide trunk. Maybe there?

The flashlight beam sweeps toward me and I duck down. But as soon as it passes, I scamper toward the big tree.

Now I can't see the officer, but I can watch the flashlight beam sweep back and forth, brightening tree trunks, which cast long narrow shadows.

And I can hear the officer's footsteps crunch over dry leaves and twigs.

I press myself against the rough bark of the big tree's trunk, my heart beating so fast it's ready to explode, and hold my breath.

The flashlight beam reaches deep into the woods around me. The urge to run makes the muscles in my legs twitch, but I can't help thinking that running may be exactly what they're hoping I'll do. They're like hunters beating the brush to flush out game. So I stay in the shadow of the tree, my heart drumming, my breaths shallow and quick.

Suddenly a radio crackles on so close to me that I jump. A staticky voice asks, "See anything?"

"Negative." The answering voice is strong and close. *Oh my God!* He must be on the other side of the tree. My heart rate and breathing speed up and I feel myself inhaling and exhaling through my lips. It's so loud that I'm certain he'll be able to hear me.

"Hold it," he says. "I thought I heard something."

In the evening of the day Katherine tricked Mia into thinking Zelda had drowned, I went online and chatted with Mia.

Cal: **U ok?**

Mia: **What do U care?**

Cal: **Im sorry. And I did tell U**.

Mia: **True. Dont U just want 2 kill her sometimes?**

Cal: **Lol! But seriously? If U feel that way, why bother with her?**

Mia: **Why do U?**

Cal: **Sometimes I wonder. But sometimes its fun. When shes not being mean. But at least shes mean 2 everyone.**

Mia: **I just wish she liked me.**

Cal: **Other people like U.**

Mia: **Some people only want what they cant have.**

Cal: **Like U and K?**

Mia: **Duh.**

The officer's flashlight beam sweeps. Any second now he'll come around the tree. I pull my breath in and duck as far down as possible. I feel the ground with my hand, and my fingers close around a stick. I throw it as hard as I can from that awkward position.

Thirty feet away the stick rustles through some branches and thumps to the ground. The flashlight beam instantly swings toward the sound and I hear the officer's footsteps go in that direction.

"See her?" the staticky voice asks through the radio.

"Naw, it must have been an animal."

"What do you want to do?" asks the voice.

"Let's go back to the cars, check in with headquarters. She could be anywhere by now."

The flashlight beam swings back toward the parking lot. I feel dizzy with relief as the officers get into their cars and drive away. Sitting behind the tree, I take deep breaths, amazed that my trick worked. But now what? Where am I going to spend the night? I have no place to go, and besides, the police are still actively searching for me. I'm probably best off staying here in the woods, where they've already looked.

And now I realize I have another problem. How did the police know I was in the old EMS building? The alert came over the scanner almost as soon as I called Slade. I know they can trace calls, but can they trace them *that* fast?

Or did Slade tip them off? What if the police have found out he helped me? What if they're forcing him to assist them, to let them know the instant I call?

"When it comes to guys, I hear you have the Tampon Attitude."

"Oh, really? What's that?"

"Use 'em once and throw 'em away."

"Very funny."

"Is it true?"

"I bet you'd love to find out, wouldn't you?"

chapter 21

Monday 4:16 P.M.

MY HEART THUDS heavily. Griffen Clemment has just gotten off a bus, lugging a heavy-looking backpack. I recognize him from the Facebook photo, but he's taller than I imagined and has a tall boy's gawkiness. I'm standing behind a hedge beside a driveway two houses down from his. Half a dozen newspapers in blue and yellow bags are scattered around the driveway, so I have a feeling whoever lives here is away.

While I hide behind the hedge, waiting, I pull the latest edition of the *Fairchester Press* out of its yellow plastic bag.

POLICE RULE OUT SEX ATTACK IN MURDER
Local Teen Still Wanted For Questioning

Soundview—Chief of Police Samuel Jenkins told reporters today that there was no evidence of sexual assault in the murder of Katherine Remington-Day late Saturday night. The seventeen-year-old Soundview High student was stabbed to death while attending a beer party in the woods behind a town baseball field.

"At this point we are still investigating the motive," the police chief stated. When asked if there were any suspects in the case, Chief Jenkins would say only that his department was eager to speak to Callie Carson, seventeen, a friend of Ms. Remington-Day's who was photographed next to the body with a blood-spattered knife in her hand.

Ms. Carson was last seen running away from the scene of the murder. The police are urging anyone with information to call the anonymous tip hotline.

Griffen is coming down the sidewalk, wearing khaki slacks, a white shirt, a school tie, and a blue blazer. Thank God he's alone, and yet I'm still terrified. I'm a complete stranger to him. If I were in his shoes, I'd probably call the police the instant I figured out who I was.

My feet feel like they're buried in cement, as if somehow they know that this is a huge mistake, even if the rest of me doesn't. But I don't know what else to do. If I don't speak to him, who will I speak to? I feel miserable, sick with anxiety and lack of sleep, tired and cold and dirty and gross after spending the night trying to sleep on the ground in the woods. Maybe part of me wants him to turn me in just so I can take a shower and sleep on something soft tonight. Maybe I want him to do what I can't bring myself to do.

He's going to pass the driveway in a second. It's now or never. Still not sure what to say, I step out from behind the hedge and clear my throat. He turns his head, glances at me, takes another step, then stops and looks again.

For a second we just stare at each other. Suddenly I'm aware of something strange that didn't come through in the Facebook photo: Griffen looks familiar. I feel like I've seen him somewhere before. But he and Slade have similar features. I mean, it would be easy to tell them apart—by height, for one thing—but at the same time they could be mistaken for brothers. Both have straight blond hair and strong chins. It strikes me as a peculiar coincidence. Do I feel like I've seen him before because he reminds me a little of Slade? Or because I really *have* seen him before? But I can't dwell on that now. Meanwhile, my heart is banging so hard I can feel my temporal artery throbbing.

I manage to issue a raspy "Please."

He scowls, says nothing, and stares.

"Do you know who I am?" I ask, trembling.

His eyes narrow.

"I'm . . . the girl everyone's looking for. I . . . I need to talk to you."

He doesn't react. This is completely unnerving. Shouldn't he be just a tad bit freaked? Everyone thinks I'm a killer. No doubt I'm the first in that category he's ever encountered.

"I didn't kill Katherine." I feel like I'm wound tight, close to snapping and unwinding into a frayed mess. "I know you have no reason to believe me, but it's true."

He blinks and takes a step backward.

"Don't go!" I beg. "Please! I just want to talk. I swear. I just want to ask you some questions."

But he's backing up, turning as if he's about to sprint away. Only that heavy, book-filled pack on his back shifts from one side to the other, and the next thing I know, Griffen Clemment trips on his own feet, topples over, and lands hard on his side in the street.

"Unnnhhhh." A long slow groan slips out through his lips and he lies on the asphalt as if stunned.

"Oh my God!" I kneel beside him. "Are you okay?"

"I . . . I don't know." His voice is higher than you'd expect, and he seems really out of it.

"Come on." I help him slide his arms out of the pack. "You can't just lie here in the middle of the street." I get him to his feet and walk him to the curb. Then I go back and get the backpack. A moment later we're sitting side by side on the curb and I'm brushing the sand and dirt off his blazer. One of his pant knees is torn and the scraped skin under it oozes dozens of little beads of blood. I pull a napkin from my jeans and dab the red away. "Does it hurt?"

"Yes."

"See if you can straighten it."

He does what I tell him. His leg goes straight and then he bends it back up without complaining or grimacing.

"Listen, Griffen, I can't sit here out in the open like this. Everyone can see us." I jerk my head back toward the hedge. "Can we go back in there? I don't think they're home."

He gives me a searching look. "You're not planning on doing anything bad to me, are you?"

It seems like a strange question from a guy who's nearly a foot taller than me, but I've begun to perceive a softness and a frailty in him. It's hard to imagine how he could have been mixed up with the likes of Dakota and Katherine. "No. I was just hoping to find out some things."

He tilts his head curiously. I get up quickly, but he takes longer, groaning and rising slowly and stiffly. We each take a strap of the backpack and lug it behind the hedge. Griffen sits down on it and dabs his knee with the napkin. I sit cross-legged on the grass and look up at him. Again I have that feeling I've seen him someplace before. I just can't figure out where.

"Last spring something happened between Katherine and Dakota and I heard you were involved," I tell him.

Big frown. "Look, no offense, but you're wanted by the police. This is a mistake. I shouldn't be talking to you." He presses his hands against the backpack as if to rise.

Desperate, I grab the sleeve of his blazer. "Have you ever been blamed for something you didn't do?" I ask, holding on. "Try magnifying that feeling about a hundred thousand times. Then add a life sentence to it."

He stares at me.

"I swear I'll never tell anyone we met," I say.

He thinks it over. I let go of his sleeve.

"So you want to know what happened with me and Dakota and Katherine?" he says. "I met Dakota at a cotillion and she seemed really interested. I mean, it was kind of weird. Like, I'm not the type who has a steady stream of girls trying to knock down the door, you know? But she was just really, like, insistent. So we started to hang out. And then somewhere along the way, she introduced me to Katherine." Griffen pauses and winces slightly. "And I mean, she . . . I mean, Katherine . . ." He shakes his head and seems to shiver. "She told me all kinds of things about Dakota that . . . sounded really bad."

"Like what?"

"Like that she was a total slut and had even been treated for an STD and that if I went out with her, I might catch something." He pauses to bend his knee and winces again.

"So what happened next?" I ask, trying to keep him on track.

"Then Katherine made this big play for me. And like I said, I'm not exactly used to that kind of attention. *And* she swore she'd never tell Dakota. And"—he shrugs—"I fell for it. And the next thing I knew, Dakota knew all about it, and she just went totally bonkers."

"So you think Katherine told Dakota?"

"Or she told someone else, who told Dakota. Doesn't really matter." Is that a trace of remorse in his voice? He can't enjoy admitting that he was duped. Still, it's incredibly helpful news, because if Katherine stole him, it gives Dakota a motive for wanting revenge. And I'm wondering about something else. "I guess the thing I don't understand is how Katherine could do that to Dakota and then two weeks later they were acting like best friends again."

"That's what happened?"

"You didn't know?"

He shakes his head. "I haven't talked to either of them. To tell you the truth, I'm totally fine with that. I mean, at first I felt pretty bad about Dakota. It was probably stupid of me to believe all that stuff about her being a slut and having STDs and all. But . . ." His voice trails off.

"But?"

He seems reluctant to say more.

"Please, if there's something I should know . . . ," I say, urging him. "Something that would help prove that I didn't kill Katherine."

"Well . . . I don't know what this'll prove, but when that whole thing happened, when Dakota found out about me and Katherine . . . I started getting some really freaky texts. The callback number was blocked, so I could never completely be sure who they were from, but I'm almost positive they were from Dakota."

"What did they say?"

"Really bizarre threatening stuff. But the thing is, like I just said, I can't *swear* they came from her. I mean, it makes sense that she's the one who sent them, and it wasn't like anyone else had a reason to send me things like that, but the police said—"

"The police? How did the police know?"

Griffen looks surprised. "We told them. I mean, the texts were totally threatening. As soon as I got them, I told my parents and they went to the police. But the cops said there was nothing they could do. They couldn't track the texts and that was that."

"That's all they said?"

"Well, they said I shouldn't tell anyone or spread any rumors, because there was no way to prove who really sent them and, you know, like, Dakota's mother is a congresswoman and people might get the wrong idea."

"Would you tell *me* what they said?"

He grimaces, as if reluctant to disobey police orders. I give him a pleading look, trying to remind him of what's at stake.

He nods. "Whoever sent the texts said they wanted to kill me. One even threatened to kill me *and* Katherine."

The news goes through me like an electric current. Maybe there's no way to prove that the texts came from Dakota. But like Griffen said, who else would have sent them?

"I don't understand why the police didn't do more to follow up on them," I tell him.

Griffen raises his eyebrows and gives me a look as if the answer is obvious. Then it hits me: Dakota's uncle, Samuel Jenkins, is the chief of police. She's his niece. Of course he wouldn't want rumors spread about her.

"Do you still have them?" I ask.

"The text messages?" Griffen shakes his head. "I mean, the police probably have the copies I printed out. But I erased them from my phone."

That's disappointing, but still, I'm pretty sure that if his parents went to the police, there's a record of a complaint. And the copies Griffen gave them of the threats. It all has to be there somewhere.

Griffen turns his head toward his house and straightens his leg again. "I better get going."

"Okay." I get up.

Griffen rises stiffly. I help him get the straps over his shoulder.

For a moment we're practically face-to-face. Again, I feel certain his is familiar.

"Have we ever seen each other before?" I ask.

He shakes his head and then walks off. But it's still bothering me.

As much as Mr. Lamont wanted Slade to work in his drywall business after high school, some kind of military service came first. It was a family tradition, a duty, going back to the First World War.

After the initial two months of National Guard training, when we weren't allowed to call each other, Slade and I would video chat a few times a week. He always tried to smile and be brave, but he wasn't a good enough actor to get away with it. His sadness, homesickness, and fear of being sent overseas always came through.

There was one exception, one night in the summer when he really did seem excited. It began with his waking me up with a phone call around one in the morning. "Get on the computer," he said when I answered.

"Why? Is something wrong? Are you okay?"

"Just do it! I have to talk to you."

Still half asleep, I staggered to my computer and slumped into the chair. A few moments later Slade came on.

"You look wide awake," he said with a smirk.

"You woke me up!" I tried to sound annoyed, but I was happy to see and speak to him, even if it was on the jumpy Internet connection.

"I know what I want to do!" he announced excitedly. "I'm going to be a commercial fisherman."

"Are you high?"

"No! I'm serious! I mean, I know I have to work with my dad when I get back, but someday that's what I'm going to be."

Since Slade and his dad loved to fish, it wasn't a totally off-the-wall idea. But it came pretty close. "Where did you come up with this?" I asked.

He told me about a guy named Rick he'd met that night in a bar near Fort Benning. Rick was in another National Guard unit and his family ran a fishing trawler out of Montauk Point on Long Island. "It was amazing, Cal. He talked about what he and his family have been doing for generations, and showed me some pictures and it was like, 'Hey! This is it! This is what I've been waiting for! It's what I've always wanted to do!' You know what I'm saying? Like after all this time of feeling like there was something else out there, but I didn't know what it was. Well, now I know!"

I thought of asking exactly how he intended to be a commercial fisherman in Soundview, or what would become of the drywall business, but it was such a joy to hear him sound excited that I couldn't rain on his parade. So I said, "That's great, Slade. And it sounds like you've found a friend, too."

I had no way of knowing that was the wrong thing to say. On the computer screen the smile left Slade's face and his voice immediately became subdued. "Well, yeah, except Rick's unit's been called up. They're being sent overseas to do support work for the troops. He leaves next month." He was quiet for a moment and I wanted to kick myself, until I thought of something that really scared me.

"Slade, do . . . you think they may call up your unit, too?"

"Right now I'd say the chances are about sixty-forty," he answered glumly.

I felt my body clench. "If you go, how long?"

"At least a year. But a lot of guys are being stop-lossed and wind up doing two tours."

That would be two years. I couldn't imagine him being away for so long. I'd be almost twenty by the time he came home. It felt like an impossibly long time. And what if he was injured or killed?

We talked a little longer, then said good-bye. I went back to bed but couldn't fall asleep. I was convinced that commercial fishing was just a whim. But what if he was sent overseas? Then what?

chapter 22

Monday 5:30 P.M.

IT'S DINNERTIME AND I'm in a convenience store with a craving for Ben & Jerry's Chocolate Fudge Brownie ice cream. The place is nearly empty, but the bright lights are unnerving. There's no place to hide in here. Cameras are mounted on the walls, and up in the corner is one of those big convex mirrors so the man behind the counter can watch. I feel like some kind of nocturnal creature that's been thrust suddenly into the sunlight.

I glance at the counter, where the clerk is watching a small TV. I'm starving and can't wait to eat, but also afraid to go up to the checkout, where yet another stranger will have an opportunity to look at my face. But I can't dawdle, as that will also attract his attention. I pick out a frosty container and head for the front.

As I get close to the cash register, I become aware of the sound of the television. A female voice reporting: "In a news conference today, Soundview Police Chief Samuel Jenkins said the police still want to speak to Callie Carson in connection with the murder two nights ago of seventeen-year-old Katherine

Remington-Day. While declining to say whether Ms. Carson is a suspect in the case, the police chief warned local citizens not to help her hide."

The scene shifts to a podium with several microphones, where Chief Jenkins stands. He's a heavyset man, almost bald on top except for some long thick strands of black hair combed straight back and held in place with gel. "We believe that Ms. Carson is still in the area. She needs food and a place to stay, so it stands to reason that someone may be sheltering her. If that's true, people need to be aware that they may be charged with rendering criminal assistance if Ms. Carson is implicated in this crime."

The scene shifts back to the TV studio and the blonde anchorwoman. In one corner of the screen is a big grainy gray blowup of my face from the yearbook. "Ms. Carson is about five feet tall and weighs around a hundred pounds. If you think you've seen her, the police have provided a phone number—"

Seeing that photo, and hearing again that I'm wanted, gives me a physical jolt. Even though hardly a second passes when I don't worry about who might be looking at me, that photo on TV kicks it all up a notch.

I'm so fixated on the TV that I don't realize that the man at the cash register has stopped watching. He's looking at me curiously, as if it's just struck him that I'm roughly the same height and weight as this person the police are looking for. I freeze, caught between opposing impulses to drop the ice cream and run and to pay as fast as I can and *then* run. Both are bad ideas. Instead, I place the container on the counter, begin searching in my pockets for money, and say, "Isn't that weird? I mean, five feet tall and a hundred pounds? That's the same as me. Well, I hope they find her, you know?"

The man blinks, then nods, takes my money, and makes change. "You want a bag for that?"

"Yeah, sure, and maybe a couple of napkins and a plastic spoon?"

"You got it."

A moment later I'm out on the sidewalk, walking away quickly but hopefully not so fast that it's noticeable. Down the block is a small park, where I settle onto a bench set close to some trees and start spooning delicious ice cream into my mouth and wondering which is more unbelievable—that I said what I said to the man behind the counter or that it seemed to work.

I have to admit that I'm pretty pleased with myself, although it does make me wonder where this talent for subterfuge comes from. When did I learn to be so devious?

Just then a police car shoots past.

When he wasn't fighting with Sebastian, Dad tended to be quiet. He worked long hours and when he came home at night, he always had a couple of drinks and watched TV. On the weekends he worked around the house or watched sports. Mom and I got to be pretty good at tiptoeing around him.

When I first started running on the cross-country team, I asked him to come to one of my meets, but he always had excuses to explain why he couldn't. Mom would come to watch if she could.

Once, in the car, going home, I asked her if Dad had played any sports in high school.

"Tennis," she said.

"Seriously?" I said. I'd never heard him mention that, and I'd never seen a tennis racket or a tennis ball anywhere in our house. "So he stopped?"

"Uh-huh."

"How come?"

"You'll have to ask him," Mom said.

But I never did.

The police car stops in front of the store where I bought the ice cream. As the officer gets out, the counterman I thought I so cleverly fooled comes out to the sidewalk and points in my direction.

By the time the officer gets back into the police car and makes a U-turn, I've scooted out of the park and am crouching down behind a Big Brothers clothing bin in the parking lot next door. But I know I can't stay here, or anywhere around town. I've been spotted and I have to believe that other officers are coming. There's a rusty chain-link fence at the back of the parking lot with a hole just large enough for me to squeeze through, onto the property that's part of the middle school.

Moments later I'm cutting through the school parking lot, keeping low and weaving between the parked cars, feeling as if the Earth's gravity has just doubled and is pressing heavily on me and making it more difficult to go forward. I'm weighed down by self-doubt. Where do I go? Where can I hide this time?

The sudden descent from overconfidence to no confidence leaves me scared, anxious, all alone in the parking lot, and all alone in the world. I'm dirty, smelly, and tired, and I don't want to hide again. I don't want to be by myself anymore. I feel so insignificant and worthless that I might just curl up in a fetal position right here between the parked cars and wait to be discovered and arrested and sent to jail forever. Maybe they'll put me in the Fishkill Correctional Facility, the same place as Sebastian. The notorious Carsons—brother-and-sister murder-and-mayhem team.

No, I forgot. Prisons aren't coed.

I hear shouting from the field behind the school. It sounds like an after-school soccer game. I know it's crazy, but right now I need those voices, ordinary people around me—otherwise I'm going to implode.

Sure enough, there's a soccer game in progress. The sidelines are filled with parents and families. The soccer field borders on a marshy area thick with tall reeds. I join the cheering crowd on the side nearest the reeds, in case I have to make a dash for freedom, and stand where I'm both part of the crowd and slightly apart from it. I just have to cling to the hope that no one is going to think that a girl on the run would be standing around watching a soccer game.

At first I'm so wrapped up in my own thoughts that I'm only vaguely aware that it's a girls' soccer game. But gradually I realize that they're not only girls but girls about the same size and age of Alyssa, Slade's little sister.

And there she is, racing around the field, her brown

ponytail bouncing. I quickly glance down the sideline to see if Slade's here. There's no sign of him on this side of the field and I look across to the people lining the other side. *Oh my God!* He's partway down the field, yelling encouragement. The pendulum of my emotions swings back toward elation, and the next thing I know, I've walked down the sideline until I'm directly across from him. Each time his eyes move in my direction, I raise my hand to shoulder height and softly wave.

But he's too involved in the game to notice. It's driving me crazy. I want to run all the way around the field and into his arms, but I might just as well start shouting to everyone that the girl the police are looking for is here.

I wave again and this time his eyes stay on me. His eyebrows dip, then shoot upward as if they're going to rocket right off his forehead. I press my finger to my lips and feel joyous. Slade looks to the left and the right and then begins to walk down the sideline toward the goal, as if he's coming around the field to me. He's a little gimpy and I can tell his knee is still bothering him.

That's when a police car shoots past the front of the school at pursuit speed, but once again with its lights and siren off. It's headed toward the entrance to the parking lot. Then tires screech to my left as another police car races up the footpath that connects the school grounds to the park next door. They're headed for the soccer field, and they've blocked both avenues of escape.

chapter 23

Monday 6:09 P.M.

MOST OF THE people on the sidelines are still cheering the soccer players, but a few are watching as the police officers get out of their cruisers and start looking around. Near the goal, Slade stops, his head turning from the police to me and back again. Meanwhile, I've backed slowly away from the crowd, toward the reeds. Everyone's so busy watching either the game or the police that no one notices that as soon as I feel the reeds at my back, I turn and step into them.

The ground turns soft and muddy. My feet sink and my shoes stick. No matter how slowly and carefully I try to go, the reeds scratch and rattle as I weave through them. As soon as I think I'm out of sight, I stop and listen, but all I hear is the crowd cheering. To the west the sun is beginning to set. Golden red light catches the cattails overhead. In the stillness of the reeds, I wonder whether the police will search the marsh and, if they do, whether I'll be able to hear them coming first.

Or will it be Slade who comes? My shoes sinking into the

mud, and chilly water seeping against my feet, I wonder if he saw me go into the reeds. If the police leave before the soccer game ends, will he come in here and find me?

I hear a rustle and my heart leaps. It's him! I swivel my head around anxiously, trying to peer through the reeds, searching for a glimpse.

And then I hear a growl.

Every muscle in my body goes rigid. I can't breathe. Now more rustling and another growl. My heart's racing.

Now a snarl so close that I don't understand why I can't see the animal making it. I turn my head in every direction. Where is it?

The fear is so intense I feel light-headed. *Oh God, Callie, whatever you do, don't faint!*

Then I see movement through the reeds.

Bared white fangs and yellow wolflike eyes.

The snarling dog with bared teeth has a brown-and-black face; the fur on its back is raised. A German shepherd. I can hardly breathe. *They've brought a police dog!*

I am frozen with fear and clench my hands so tight that for a moment I don't realize that the pain I'm feeling is from my own fingernails digging into my palms. Big dogs have always terrified me. And no big dog scares me more than a German shepherd. This one probably weighs more than I do. Its long teeth and ferocious growl make me want to cry out for help. Suddenly I can't wait for the police to get here and arrest me. Anything as long as they take this dog away. *Please!*

The dog has stopped four feet from me. As our eyes lock I wait for the crash of the police officers through the reeds.

But all I hear are parents yelling and cheering for their children. The dog snarls but doesn't come closer. I stay frozen, my feet now icy cold and soaked in muddy water. The sun is still setting, the light grayish and filtered. Where are the police? Why aren't they coming?

But wait. Does Soundview even have a K9 unit? I don't remember ever seeing one before. Is it possible this isn't a police dog?

I've hardly completed the thought when a woman calls, "Franklin! Here boy! Franklin!"

Without taking its yellow eyes off me, the shepherd perks up its ears.

"Come on, Franklin!"

Franklin's fur relaxes. The teeth disappear under the snout. He turns and trots away. A rushing wave of relief leaves me feeling light-headed. Instinctively I squat down and close my hands tightly around the base of some stalks to steady myself.

"Shrimp?" A voice, hardly more than a whisper, comes through the reeds.

Except for that one time when Slade excitedly announced that he wanted to become a commercial fisherman, our video chats were gloomy and depressing, with Slade going on and on about how much he hated being at Fort Benning, how lonely he was, and how worried he was about being sent overseas. It got to the point where I began to dread speaking to him and wished he wouldn't tell me everything he was thinking and feeling. I certainly wasn't doing the same. I didn't tell him about the fun I was having with

Katherine and her crowd, and I definitely didn't say anything about the pressure from Katherine to break up with him.

But not being honest made me feel guilty, and it was hard to hide that guilt when we were face-to-face on our computers. By August I was making excuses to speak to him on the phone instead of video chatting. But that just meant more lies and made me feel even worse.

"What's wrong?" he asked one night on the phone when I said my computer was acting up.

"Nothing."

"Come on, Cal. You told me two weeks ago your computer was broken. You're telling me it's still broken?"

I didn't know how to answer. I was sick of hearing myself make up excuses and lies.

"Cal, be honest. Tell me what's going on," he urged.

What I could be honest about were my feelings. "I miss you. I wish you'd come home. It's hard when you're so far away."

"What's hard?" he asked. "Staying faithful? Not going out with other guys?"

"No!" I gasped, stung by the accusation. "Nothing like that! What makes you say that?"

"The three Ps," he said.

I had no idea what he was talking about. "What?"

"It's something they teach in the army. To succeed and survive you need patience, perseverance, and paranoia. When I first heard that, I understood the patience and perseverance right away, but paranoia? Who wants you to be paranoid? But they say if you want to survive in war, that's how you have to be."

"This isn't war."

"Right. But you know what? Part of war is survival, and right now I feel like I'm fighting for the survival of Cal and Slade. Because my gut is telling me something is wrong, and paranoia is telling me that it's more than just a broken computer. It's already happened twice in my unit."

"What's happened?"

"The e-mail comes. The one from the girlfriend saying it's over. That can't happen to us, Cal. It'll kill me."

"I haven't seen anyone," I said.

"You sure?"

I don't know why that question bothered me so much. Maybe because his neediness felt like more pressure on me.

"I think I'd know if I was seeing someone," I said. But even as I said it, I felt my insides twist with guilt, because Slade's instincts were right. It wasn't another guy I was seeing, but another life, one that promised to be a lot more fun and carefree than the one I was having with him.

Instead of accepting my reply, Slade pressed again. "I need to know that I don't have to worry about that, Cal. Not with us. You need to promise me."

Something inside me snapped. "Or what? God, Slade, you make it sound like your whole life depends on me. I can't stand feeling like I'm the only thing responsible for your happiness. I want to have some happiness, too. I'm only seventeen, for God's sake. Is this what I've got to look forward to for the rest of my life? Because if it is, no thanks."

I hung up.

chapter 24

Monday 6:17 P.M.

WE STAND IN the muddy, cold shadows of the reeds. The cheers
are still coming from the soccer field.

"What were you doing there?" he asks.

"I just . . . I don't know. . . . They spotted me in town and I
had to run. Then I felt so scared and alone, and so tired of hiding.
I just wanted to be near people. And then I saw you."

He looks at my face, clearly puzzled. "Are those real?"

For a second I don't know what he's talking about. Then I
pull the ring off my lip and he smiles as if he's relieved, then
shakes his head. "Did you *have* to cut off your hair?"

"Yes."

"What happened last night? You disappeared in the middle
of our conversation." It sounds like he really cares, like he
was worried about me. Just knowing that is like breathing in pure
oxygen. It makes me feel hopeful and reenergized.

"I couldn't stay on," I tell him. "The police were coming.
They must be tracing my phone. But I have to tell you what I've

learned." I tell him about Griffen Clemment. "He thinks Dakota sent those text threats. So you see, Slade? She *did* have a motive for killing Katherine."

He draws in a breath and for a moment I wonder if he's going to argue that girls don't go around killing their friends just because one stole another's boyfriend. But he doesn't know Dakota. Then again, a week ago I might have argued the same thing, and I *do* know her. It's just that you learn things and start to put together the pieces and that's when the seemingly impossible begins to look possible.

"Listen . . . ," he begins.

t you're going to say, Slade," I say, cutting him

n't." He cuts *me* short. "The police came to my erviewed me for a long time. I had to tell them

unexpected jolt, but I know immediately that I prised.

"They interviewed you about me?"

"Not just you. Everything." He looks down at our muddy feet. "Almost made me feel like they thought I was a suspect."

"You think they do that just to make sure you're telling the truth?" I ask.

He shrugs and shakes his head. My mood begins to plummet again. They were bound to get to him sooner or later. It feels like the police are getting closer and closer. I must be crazy to think I can skulk around this town, trying to prove that Dakota killed Katherine, when everyone's looking for me.

* * *

I'd never hung up on Slade before. I sat there, feeling a crazy storm of emotions rage inside me. Anger, relief, guilt, resentment. Was I facing a choice? Tedium with Slade or fun with Katherine? Security or uncertainty?

The phone rang again. "Hi," I said.

"I'm sorry," he said. "You're right. It's not fair to dump all this on you."

"I shouldn't have hung up on you," I said.

"I love you, Cal."

"I love you, Slade." I believed it in my head, but it wasn't what I was feeling in my heart.

chapter 25

Monday 6:22 P.M.

I SUDDENLY REALIZE that there are no more cheers coming from the soccer field. It's now nearly dark and the game must be over. Slade glances over his shoulder. "I have to get back."

"Okay." I hate to see him go, but Alyssa must be wondering where he is.

He doesn't leave me just yet. "Still think you can prove Dakota did it?"

"I don't know, but what other choice do I have?"

He nods. "Okay." Then he's gone, and once again I'm all alone.

By the time it's dark enough for me to leave the marsh, my teeth are chattering and my wet feet feel numb. I walk down a quiet street and pass houses with windows lit, houses in which I know families are gathering around kitchen tables for dinner even if I can't see them.

"The higher-ups say the reason we're there is to bring those people freedom. But just about every guy who's been over there says the

same thing: the people don't want us there to help them be free.
They don't want us there, period."

"*I know. It's a terrible situation.*"

"*I just don't see the point in it.*"

"*I wish I could help you.*"

Sometimes I wondered if Mia was only interested in me because she wanted to know why Katherine seemed to favor me over her.

Mia: **Did U ask Y she didnt invite me 2 the city?**

Cal: **Told U I cant ask things like that**

Mia: **It really bothers me**

Cal: **Y not just make other friends?**

Mia: **Know what Groucho Marx once said?**

Cal: **???**

Mia: **Hed never join a club that would let a person like him be a member.**

Cal: **LOL ?**

Mia: **Like, we only want what we cant have**.

Cal: **But shes so mean 2 U.**

Mia: **Things change.**

At Umbrella Point I use Slade's penlight to search around under the umbrella until I find the note I knew my mother would leave for me.

You have to go to the police. Hiding from them just
makes you look guilty. Please, Callie. We'll find a way to get

a lawyer. We'll prove you're innocent. Where are you staying? What are you eating? I'm so worried about you. Please, honey, do the right thing.

Love, Mom

It's what you'd expect from a mother. I leave an answer, this one saying I'm okay but I can't do what she's asked and someday I'll explain why.

And now it's time to go see Jerry.

"This is the perfect time to dump him," Katherine said one day last summer when a bunch of us were in the Apple Store at the mall.

"Why?" I asked, amazed at her nerve.

"Because he isn't here," she said as if it were obvious. "You don't have to worry about him making a big scene. If you do it now, by the time he gets back, he'll be over it."

By the time he gets back . . . Those words echoed eerily in my head. So Katherine remembered the night I confessed my secret fear about Slade's being sent overseas.

Now she leaned close and dropped her voice. "Don't you want to be part of the inner circle?"

I'd heard passing reference to the IC before. Mia seemed to think it was some kind of secret society, but when I asked her what she thought it was for, she admitted that she didn't know.

"What is it?" I asked.

Katherine gestured at Mia and Kirsten, then gave me a conspiratorial smile. "It's what *they're* not in."

chapter 26

Monday 6:57 P.M.

JERRY FAIRMAN WAS Sebastian's best friend, and as strange and mercurial as Sebastian is, Jerry is stranger still, a reclusive techno-whiz freak geek who rarely leaves his parents' house. I know I'm taking a chance by going to see him, but at this point anything I do means taking a chance. Besides, Jerry isn't the sort of person who deals well with authority, and conspiracy theories are like catnip to him. I remember at Sebastian's nineteenth birthday party, Jerry cornered me and went on and on about how this country never actually sent men to the moon, and how the moon landings were faked on a Hollywood movie set to give the Russians the impression of America's great superiority in space.

Of course, he also believes that UFOs exist and that the air force knows all about them. But the most disturbing thing he ever told me was about something called the New World Order, which he said was headquartered in a secret city under the Denver International Airport and run by the wealthiest and most powerful men in the world, who controlled everything and had ordered the destruction of the World Trade Center towers on 9/11 to drive up the price of oil.

Now *that's* extreme.

I don't know what to expect as I tiptoe through the dark around the back of the Fairman house. The basement light is on. I bend down and tap my knuckles gently against the glass, hoping it will be just loud enough for Jerry to hear and not alert the rest of the household. A few moments later a shadow appears on the floor and then I see Jerry's pale face as he peers up, squinting and frowning, with no trace of recognition.

Afraid of being overheard, I lean closer to the glass. "It's Callie," I say in a low voice. The frown on Jerry's face deepens. It's hard to imagine that there is anyone in Soundview who is so detached from the outside world that he doesn't know about Katherine's murder. But if such a person could exist, it would be Jerry.

"Callie," I repeat, a little more loudly. "Sebastian's sister." I slide the fake hoop off my lower lip. On the other side of the window, Jerry squints, blinks with astonishment, then motions to the semi-subterranean door beside the window. I go down three mold-darkened concrete steps to the screen door. It's locked. Jerry opens the inside door and gives me a perplexed look through the screen.

"Did you hear about Katherine?" I ask.

He nods.

"I was set up. Someone wanted to make it look like I killed

her. I came here because I need your help to prove I'm innocent. The person who set me up is hoping everyone will think I'm just like my brother."

I've made it sound like a conspiracy, and Jerry nods in complicity. I reach down to the latch on the screen door and jiggle it to show him it's locked. Jerry's eyes travel down and then back up. His forehead furrows. "You want to come in?"

"I need help, Jerry. There's no one else I can go to."

It's easy to picture the gears grinding in Jerry's head. He could be hesitating for any number of reasons. "What do you want from me?" he asks.

"I'm having a problem with texting and cell phones. I thought maybe you could help."

There's nothing he likes more than fixing techy problems. To him it's a form of recreation. Relief floods through me as he reaches down and unlocks the latch, then gestures me in and points at the floor, where shoes and boots are lined in an orderly row. I take off my wet shoes and socks . . . but now he looks at my bare feet and makes a face.

"I had to go through a marsh," I explain.

Someone else might go get me a pair of dry socks, but Jerry doesn't think that way. Instead, he pulls a bottle of Purell out of his pocket and gestures for me to cup my hands so he can squeeze some onto my palms. He waits while I rub the gel into my hands; then he nods down at my bare feet.

Yes, he's serious, and I'm not in a position to argue. So I do what he wants and then follow him into his room.

It's a shrine to OCD. Everything is in its place—books, in

neat alphabetical order, computers, screens, printers, hard drives, phone-docking station, fax machine, tools. In two corners of the room, air purifiers hum and emit an antiseptic scent. The basement feels like a cross between a hospital operating room and a nuclear command post, and at its center is a high-backed black leather office chair and a desk with four computer screens stacked two and two. On two of the screens are cyber representations of green oval card tables with gambler avatars. On the third screen is a street scene from Second Life with voluptuous female avatars in skintight clothes and muscular young male avatars with cyber testosterone coursing through their veins. On the fourth is an episode of *South Park*.

Jerry watches me uncomfortably while I gaze around. It's clear that the source of his discomfort isn't that I'm a suspect in Katherine's murder but that I'm standing in his private inner sanctum, where so few have been allowed over the years.

"Okay if I sit?" I ask.

He tilts his head uncertainly, then pulls an empty blue plastic milk crate from a corner and flips it over. I sit down and he slides into the leather office chair and quickly studies the screens of the poker games. With rapid movements he adjusts his mouse and flicks his keyboard.

"So if you didn't do it, who did?" His bluntness catches me by surprise. Social graces were never his strong suit. Still, it's a logical question. I don't want to tell him what I suspect, so I just say I'm not sure but I'm following some leads. He looks askance at me, and I continue. "I know that must make you wonder if I'm lying. I'd probably be more believable if I said I had no idea, but I do have an idea. I just don't want to say right now."

His gaze stays on me, making me feel uncomfortable. Finally he glances at the screens, makes some more adjustments. "So you said you had some kind of problem?"

"About six months ago someone sent anonymous text messages to someone I know. He erased them from his phone. Is there any way to track down those messages and find out what they said?"

Without taking his eyes from his screens, Jerry shakes his head. "They're gone. Phone companies can't store content. It's not only a privacy issue but a logistical nightmare. "

He moves the mouse, still playing two poker games at once. The games may exist in the ethereal world of cyberspace, but the money involved is cold hard cash. When that public defender wanted my brother to cop an attempted manslaughter plea and do eighteen to twenty-five years, Jerry paid for the lawyer who got the sentence down to eight to fifteen. The money came from online gambling.

"That's all you wanted to know?" he asks, and I can't help getting the feeling that he's a little disappointed that I didn't bring a more exciting techno challenge for him to solve. But there's another one.

"When I turn on my phone and make a call, the police show up. I assume they're tracing my calls."

"Yeah, they trace the pings through the phone company and know what tower you're near. And if your phone has GPS, they pretty much know *exactly* where you are."

"How do I know if my phone has GPS?"

Jerry tugs a couple of Purell wipes out of a container, lays them flat on his palm, then extends his hand to me. I place my phone on the wipes and watch while he swipes the outside of it, then carefully opens it and wipes the inside. At no point does he touch the phone with his bare fingertips. Once the phone is completely germ free, he quickly inspects it and shakes his head. "Not this piece of junk."

It may be a piece of junk, but I suspect that it's good news that there's no GPS. "So if I use it, the police just know the area I'm in, but not exactly *where* I am?"

"Right. Unless you're moving. Then they can track you from tower to tower and triangulate." He pauses and stares down at the phone. "I can make this untraceable if you want."

"Really?" I didn't expect that. "How?"

"Easy." He pries off the back and removes a small green-and-white card, which he slides into something that looks like an overgrown memory stick. He pauses momentarily to review his positions in the poker games, then plugs the thing into a USB port. In a flash the Second Life scene is replaced by computer gobbledygook. It looks a little like the green symbols from *The Matrix*, only they're not flowing; they're long multicolor lines on a white background. Jerry begins typing and working the mouse, causing numbers and values to change in the long equations.

A few seconds later he replaces the card in my phone, tosses it back to me, and once again levels his gaze in my direction. There's something in his eyes that makes me feel uncomfortable. I wish I knew what he was thinking.

"I heard you quit the cross-country team," he says.

It's a strange thing to bring up at this moment, but then, that's Jerry. "Between school and work and going up to Fishkill to see Sebastian once a week, I just couldn't do it."

He nods. "So you . . . want to take a shower? Get cleaned up?"

I feel dirty and gritty and would love to take a shower, but there's something about taking off my clothes in this house, with Jerry around, even with the bathroom door locked, that makes me uneasy.

"You need a place to stay? Want to stay here tonight?" he adds.

I do need a place to stay, but again, I feel uncomfortable. I don't know what he's thinking. He may be an antisocial recluse, but he's still a male. "I better not."

He continues to stare. "You still with that Slade guy?"

How does he know about Slade and me? And how should I answer? "Kind of."

"Kind of?" he repeats with a smile. For a moment I worry that he might take that as some sort of invitation, but then he turns back to the computer screens and resumes playing poker, and I feel relieved.

It's a strange moment. I stare at the back of Jerry's chair. All I can see are the bottoms of his calves and his shoes. I came here for help and information, but now what? I know that somewhere the phone company has a record of those anonymous texts being sent, even if they don't know what each text said. I know I have a phone I can use. But night has come and it's dark outside. Where can I go? The big leather chair squeaks as Jerry turns to face me. He has a curious but wary look. Is he wondering why I'm still here?

"Jerry, I . . . I really appreciate you helping me."

He intertwines his fingers as if in prayer and sucks in his lower lip pensively. "I heard the police are warning people that they can get in trouble for sheltering you."

I nod and stare at the floor. Is he implying that since he's taken a big risk for me, I should do something for him? Some alarm in my head is telling me it's time to go. It's hard to get up and leave this warm, dry basement, but I'm just not comfortable.

I head for the door. He follows, watching as I stuff the wet socks into my hoodie and pull the damp shoes over my bare feet. "Thanks, Jerry."

"Hey, stay in touch, okay?" he says. "And if you need any-thing . . ."

"Right, thanks." I reach for the screen door and let myself out into the night. Behind me, Jerry cleans the doorknob with a wipe.

In the cool night air, I have to decide what to do next. A harvest moon has started to rise, big and orange-red, and as I pause to look at it, I catch some movement out of the corner of my eye. It's come through the window of the basement, where Jerry has taken his seat again. His cell phone is pressed to his ear, and his expression implies that he's speaking urgently. I wish I knew to whom, and what he is saying.

I glance at the moon again and now I notice something else: near the back of the yard is a tree lit by moonlight, and in the branches is a square dark silhouette—a tree house. Stepping closer, I see planks of wood hammered crookedly into the trunk for steps. The tree house is a wooden box with a doorway and some rectangular cutouts for windows. I wonder if this is something Jerry's father built long ago in an unsuccessful attempt to get his son to go outside.

It's as good a place as any to spend the night.

A moment later, sitting in the tree house, I try Slade's number but get his recording. I don't want to leave a message. Even if the police can no longer trace my phone, they might be able to identify my voice and charge Slade with helping me.

Fatigue drifts in like a thick fog. I would like to stay awake and try to figure out what my next move should be, but instead, I lie down on the floor and close my eyes.

By August, Katherine was no longer nagging me to break up with Slade. I assumed she now liked me enough not to make it a condition of our friendship. I was being included in everything the IC did and, except for work, having the best summer of my life. And while I missed Slade, I also felt strangely liberated—free to do whatever I chose on my days and nights off, not having to feel responsible for propping him up when he sank into one of his moods.

Then, all of a sudden, it got quiet. I sent Katherine a text and got no reply. I sent an e-mail: same thing. I assumed she was on vacation.

One afternoon Mia came into the Baskin-Robbins. "So I hear you're all going to Zelda's beach house for the weekend," she said while I scooped out a double mint Oreo cone for her.

I managed to catch myself before blurting out that I didn't know what she was talking about. Mia studied me. "You don't want to talk about it because you don't want to make me feel bad, right? But it's okay. Maybe I don't care anymore."

"Really?" I asked as I handed her the cone. It was hard to imagine her changing so dramatically.

Mia leaned closer to the ice-cream case and lowered her voice. "Well, maybe I do, but I'm not going to *act* like I do anymore. I think if you act like you don't care, like Zelda and Jodie, Katherine respects you more."

I knew that worked for Zelda and Jodie, but I wasn't so sure it would work for Mia.

"Besides," she went on with a smile, "guess what? I've discovered there's actually life *outside* Soundview High."

I grinned. But as soon as she left, I called Jodie and asked if Katherine was away.

"No," she answered.

An awkward silence followed. I was suddenly filled with uncertainty. Finally I said, "I've e-mailed and texted and she hasn't answered."

"Oh, yeah," Jodie said. "Well . . . you know."

"Sorry?" I didn't know what she was talking about.

"She wanted you to do something and you didn't do it."

Even then it took a moment for me to realize what Jodie was talking about. I was stunned. All I could say was "Why is it so important to her?"

"You're asking me?" Jodie laughed. "Who knows? For all I know, maybe she wants you for herself."

chapter 27

Tuesday 6:08 A.M.

"I CAN HELP you get what you want."

"But there's a catch, right? Something I'll have to do for you?"

"Of course."

"So what is it?"

"When the time is right, I'll let you know."

I wake to a roar in my ears and sit up, disoriented. It sounds like a jet engine. The air in the tree house is heavy with moisture, and here and there water drips in through the slats of the roof. A downpour thunders from above. I check my cell phone for the time—just after six in the morning—and debate whether to call Slade, who is a late sleeper. Giving in to urgency, I call, knowing that it will surely wake him.

"Hello?" He picks up right away.

"You're up!"

"Haven't been getting much sleep lately. What's going on? Where are you? I thought you were worried the police were tracing your calls."

"Jerry fixed it so they can't trace me."

"Jerry?"

"Sebastian's old friend. I've told you about him. Crazy reclusive tech whiz?"

"Oh, yeah. So where are you? Can I see you? There's something I want to tell you."

"Uh . . ." I'm about to tell him where I am when I catch myself. What if the police are listening to *his* phone . . . or sitting there in the room with him, threatening to arrest him if he doesn't help them? "Can't you tell me over the phone?"

"I . . . No, I've been thinking, Cal, and this is something I have to tell you in person."

I feel myself fill with apprehension. "Why? What is it?"

"It's better if it's face-to-face."

I can't imagine why he can't tell me over the phone. It doesn't feel right. "Slade, it would be better if you just tell me now."

"Come on, Cal, can't you just tell me where you are? I can probably be there in five minutes. I'll explain everything when I see you."

After everything that's happened, I can't help feeling suspicious and cautious. I want to trust him, but some sixth sense is sending me warning signals. They might be about him, or they might be about something else. I only know I have to be extra careful. Paranoid, just like he said. "Slade, it's better if you tell me over the phone. Really, it's okay. No one's listening."

"I know no one's listening," he snaps, suddenly becoming angry. "Why can't you just cooperate for once? Why do you always have to have everything your way?"

"Slade, it's not that. . . . You know it isn't."

"Yeah, yeah." His words seethe with sarcasm.

"It's true!" I insist, stung.

"Right. Just like the reason you broke up with me had nothing to do with the fact that I wasn't going to college. Or I didn't know the right way to hold a fork and that my family didn't belong to the right clubs. Damn, I've heard this all before. Why do I even bother?"

"Slade, what are you talking about?" I'm truly bewildered. I can't remember ever talking to him about forks or belonging to clubs.

"Forget it, Cal."

"Forget what?"

"I said forget it. Oh, and listen, your cover's been blown. On the news last night they had a security-camera shot of you in some grocery store in your punk getup. You can bet it'll be on the local news again this morning and all over the Internet."

The anger and sarcasm hurt. "Thank you for telling me that, Slade," I say, even though I already know. "I wish you'd tell me why you're so upset."

Silence. And then, sounding choked up, he says, "Forget it, Cal. It probably doesn't even matter at this point."

"It *does* matter, Slade. Don't you want us to get back together?"

The line goes quiet. Is he still there? "Slade?"

"I . . . I gotta go, Cal."

"No!"

But he's gone.

Jodie told me why I hadn't been invited to Zelda's beach house, and why Katherine had suddenly become silent. And that was when I panicked and gave into impulse and acted rashly.

I called Slade . . . and told him it was over.

As soon as I got off the phone, I sent a text to Katherine:
I did it.

Not ten minutes passed before a text arrived from Zelda:
Want 2 go 2 my beach house this wknd?

I went, trying not to think about what I'd done, and to be honest, I had a great time. Zelda's house was huge, bright, and breezy, and the crash of the surf was always in my ears, and the fresh scent of salt air in my nose. It was Katherine, Jodie, Zelda, Brianna, and me. Dakota was away on vacation with her parents.

I felt like a different person. At night we went to a dance club, where college guys hit on us. It made me wonder if I should apply to a four-year school in the fall. Given the alternative—two years at FCC, living at home, hanging around the same old town— why not at least try to get in somewhere else? I was in a new place—with my girlfriends and with my life. By the end of the weekend, I believed Katherine. I might have loved Slade, but he wasn't right for me.

And, I thought, I was in the IC.

chapter 28

OUTSIDE, THE DOWNPOUR has eased to a drizzle. After that phone call, I can only assume that something with Slade has changed, even if I don't know what it is. All I know is that calling him back to argue or plead isn't going to solve anything. Still, I wish he hadn't gotten angry. I really wish he'd told me he loved me. Could that be why he wanted to see me in person?

And some good news came out of our conversation: Jerry really did make my phone untraceable. From the tree house, I can see the streets in front of and behind the Fairman house, and there are no police cruisers racing up with their lights and sirens off.

But now what? My disguise is no good. I am hungry and dirty and hate the way my hair and scalp feel. Is it time to turn myself in and tell the police what I've learned about the anonymous threatening texts? Wouldn't they have to look into that? Especially since they must have a record of Griffen's parents' report. At least then I'd be able to rest and eat and take a shower.

But there's that other Callie. The one who made me run even when I got the most painful stitch in my side. The one who said that no matter how many reasons I came up with for stopping, I'd still be quitting. Sometimes I hate that girl. Life would be so much simpler if she weren't there making me feel bad and guilty every time I thought about taking a shortcut or the easy way out.

I can't prove I didn't kill Katherine by hiding. So I have to think, figure out what the next step should be. There must be information out there that can help me, even if I don't know what it is or where to look for it. But I'm sure of one thing—I won't come across it if I turn myself in.

So the first thing I have to do is listen to the other Callie and not give up. And then what? To prove that someone committed murder, you have to prove that they had the opportunity, the means, and the motive.

The opportunity was at the kegger. The means was the knife. The mo—

And that's when it hits me. *The knife!* It had that square red logo with the white stick figures. The same logo I saw that day in Dakota's kitchen! I can't believe it took me this long to put it together! That will prove Dakota did it!

After the weekend at Zelda's, the fun continued for the final two weeks of the summer. Wherever the IC went and whatever they did, I was included. Not all the girls were there. Zelda stayed at the beach and Dakota was still away with her family. But that left Katherine, Brianna—who in Dakota's absence had become Katherine's constant companion—Jodie, and me.

Sometimes it was a little awkward, like when they went clothes shopping and I couldn't afford much for myself. Meanwhile, as the day Slade was due to finish Guard training and come home approached, I began to watch the local news and check the paper. Then I read this one morning in the *Fairchester Press*:

FAIRCHESTER—COUNTY OFFICIALS ANNOUNCED TODAY THAT FAIRCHESTER'S EIGHTY NATIONAL GUARD MEMBERS WILL BE DEPLOYED TO AFGHANISTAN IN LATE SEPTEMBER.

County Administrator Kevin Parsons is hoping residents will give them a patriotic send-off. The Guard members will serve as support for US Army troops.

"We're asking folks to let these men and women know how much they are appreciated," Parsons said, then added that he has asked local municipalities to fly extra American flags and put up other patriotic decorations.

Parsons, who himself is a member of a National Guard Special Forces group, said he hoped local residents would also display flags and other symbols of support. "Anyone who puts himself in harm's way for our national security deserves all the appreciation we can muster."

I felt my heart sink. Slade's worst fear had come true.

* * *

Slade was scheduled to come home the day before school started. I assumed that the men in his unit would be allowed a few weeks after training to see their families and make arrangements before their deployment. As the day of his arrival grew nearer, I became miserable and anxious and scared. Part of me yearned to see him, and part of me was terrified of what might happen if I did.

The easiest thing to do was avoid the whole issue. There were always parties on the night before school began. I joined Katherine, Brianna, Jodie, and Zelda, who volunteered to be our designated driver, because she was taking an antibiotic for an ear infection and wasn't allowed to drink.

Nobody said a word about Dakota. I knew she must have gotten home from her family vacation, but I didn't ask why she wasn't with us.

There was lots of drinking and catching up with friends we hadn't seen over the summer. By our third stop, things began to get a little fuzzy for me. I remember getting out of the car and stumbling slightly over the curb. Katherine caught my arm to steady me and we laughed at my klutziness. The next thing I knew, we were holding hands and walking across the lawn toward the next party.

"Wasn't Slade supposed to come home today?" she asked.

"Yes," I answered, surprised she knew that.

"Have you seen him?"

I shook my head.

"Do you want to?"

I shrugged. "It's probably better if I don't. He's going overseas in a few weeks."

"So you're not sorry you broke up with him?"

In my heart I knew I was very sorry. In my head I wasn't sure. But what good would it do to tell Katherine that? In her opinion I'd done the right thing by breaking up with him. "No," I said. "You were right."

Katherine squeezed my hand and then let go.

As it got late, people began to settle down. By then we were at the home of Alex Craft, the impossibly cute star of many PACE productions, playing flip cup and drinking. Then someone suggested we play suck and blow. We all sat in a circle, boy-girl-boy-girl, and started to pass a card around with our lips. You're not allowed to touch the card with your hands, and the way you keep it on your lips is by sucking in air behind it. Then you turn to the person next to you and they press their lips to the other side of the card and you blow while they suck, and the card stays with them. You're out of the game if you drop the card before you give it to the next person. And if it falls while you're getting it from or giving it to someone, you usually wind up kissing them.

I was sitting with Alex on my right and Seth Phillips on my left. The first few times Alex passed the card to me, I instantly dropped it. Our lips touched, but it didn't feel much like a kiss. And each time, I had to back out of the circle and wait for the next round to begin.

At first there was the expected protesting from the boys when their lips touched, and giggling from the girls, but it seemed like after a while, it got quieter, except when someone made a wise-crack and people laughed. Of course, the card wasn't the only thing being passed around. So was a bottle.

I don't know how long we played. People kept changing their seats and moving around. Either because I'd had so much to drink or because I had the least practice, I was usually one of the first to be DQ'd. That made me want to try harder, even though everything felt like it began to spin whenever I closed my eyes.

And then David Sloan dropped the card, and the next time it came around, Katherine got it and turned to me.

And when she tried to press the card against my lips, it fell.

And then she was pressing her lips against mine.

And I kind of remember thinking that was strange and didn't she realize that she'd dropped the card?

But her lips stayed on mine.

And then they parted.

I remember thinking, *Wait . . . no.* I might have even said it out loud, or maybe not, because as I pulled away, she leaned forward so she was still kissing me.

I'm pretty sure that at that point I turned my face away and I tried to get up, but I tripped over something.

And then I was on my hands and knees on the floor.

And then I was sick.

The next morning, my first as a senior in high school, I had the worst hangover of my life. But I took a bunch of Advil and went anyway. At lunch we took our seats at the same table we'd sat at the past year, only Dakota wasn't there and it was now Brianna who sat closest to Katherine.

Everyone chatted and acted as if nothing unusual had happened the night before. They were so normal, in fact, that I began to wonder if something had really happened or I'd only imagined it.

chapter 29

Tuesday 7:43 A.M.

I WAIT INSIDE the tree house until the next downpour begins and then climb down and walk through the heavy rain, hoping that as long as it's pouring, pedestrians will be preoccupied with staying dry and trying to avoid puddles. If I'm lucky, drivers will be watching for other cars, not fugitives from the law. A pickup truck goes past, wipers swiping, and I do a double take. It's Slade and there's someone small in the passenger seat. He's driving Alyssa to school.

The Lamonts keep a spare key under a flowerpot near the back door. By the time I let myself in, I'm soaked to the skin. It's quiet and still inside. Even better, it's warm and dry. But being in this kitchen stirs up a stew of memories and emotions. There's a feeling of familiarity but also a yearning for that time when I felt like I belonged here, when I'd make a big steaming pot of spaghetti on the old stove and pretend that I was part of the family.

But this isn't the time for memories and regrets; I have to keep moving. I leave my wet shoes by the door, grab a garbage bag from under the sink, and dash up the stairs to the bathroom.

What I see in the mirror is revolting. The black hair dye has started to run down my face and neck. The makeup is streaked and smudged. *What a mess!* After stripping out of my soaked, dirty clothes, I go through my pockets for money, Slade's penlight, and other things I don't want to forget. All the change in my pockets comes to a little over a dollar. I thought I had more, but now that's just one more problem I'll have to deal with.

I stuff the wet clothes into the garbage bag and get into the shower. The hot water feels so good. It takes a lot of shampoo to get most of the black dye out. Finally I towel off and blow-dry my hair. Not all the color is out, but enough to make my hair look an unnatural shade of dirty blonde.

Wrapped in the towel, I head back downstairs and raid the kitchen. There's milk in the refrigerator, and Honey Nut Cheerios in the cupboard. Two bowls later I'm back upstairs. Alyssa's room is a reflection of a girl with one foot in the smooth sands of childhood and the other on the rocky shore of adolescence. Posters of singers on pink walls, an electric guitar leaning against a dollhouse, a training bra lying in the pile of yesterday's soccer uniform. I go through her dresser and find a long-sleeved white cotton turtleneck that will cover the Sharpie tattoo on my neck. Next I pull on denim shorts over white leggings, then a pink hoodie and a matching pink baseball cap. A pair of pink-and-white Velcro sneakers are a nice touch. Even Alyssa, at age twelve, probably wouldn't be caught dead in something so childish.

I find her old eyeglasses in a drawer and lollipops in the candy jar in the kitchen.

Standing in front of the full-length mirror, I'm almost un-nerved by how young I look. Maybe it's the candy-cane eyeglass frames, but I wonder if I'm actually more convincing as a pre-pubescent girl than I was as a punk. I wander away from the mirror and into the hall, barely conscious of where my feet are taking me until I stop outside Slade's door. So far I can justify sneaking into the Lamonts' house, eating their food, taking a shower, and borrowing some of Alyssa's clothes. Desperate times call for desperate measures. But what I want to do next crosses the line. Only I can't help myself. I press my fingers against the door to Slade's room and go in.

My heart thuds and the ache returns, stronger than ever. So little in this room has changed. The car and motorcycle posters on the wall. The ankle weights on the floor, which Slade is sup-posed to use to keep the muscles around his knee fit. The shelf of dusty everyone-gets-one trophies from soccer and Little League.

But there's something new hanging on the closet door—a pale green-gray military camouflage uniform. And on the floor, tan lace-up boots. Slade's uniform.

On his desk is a new laptop, which he got through the army PX. A photo is taped to the outer edge of the screen so that every time he sits down he sees it. It's a photo I know well, because I have a framed copy of it on my night table at home. In it Slade and I are together, arm in arm, smiles on our faces one night last April at a party Dakota gave.

I feel a rush of hope. He's kept the photo where he can see it all the time! My spirits lift. So he does still care!

Only now I notice something else in the photo. Something I

missed before, because I've always been content to look at Slade and me standing in front of the small crowd of people with drinks and food in their hands. In that crowd, staring at us with an unmistakable look of dismay on her face, is Dakota.

And suddenly I have an outrageous idea. Or maybe the best word to describe it is *desperate*. Jerry has made my phone untraceable. So that means I can call . . . Dakota. I can confront her with what I think, and see how she reacts.

I go over and over it in my head, but there's so much I can't predict . . . other than the one thing I'm sure of—that I can't hide from the police much longer. That sooner or later I'm going to get caught.

With shaking hands, I turn on my phone. It's the middle of the school day, so I can't call her. But I can text. My trembling fingers make mistake after mistake. Finally I manage to get it right: **I no U killed K.**

With my heart pounding as if I've just run five miles, I hit SEND.

Now what?

I sit on Slade's bed. Even though the rain's passed, I can't go anywhere in my new disguise, because it's a weekday and girls my age should be in school. So I have no choice but to wait. But I know that it won't be long before Dakota reads the text. It's the middle of fourth period at school. Even if she has gym or is super busy in some class, the period ends at 10:56 and she'll read it then.

The first week of senior year passed and Dakota was still a

no-show at lunch in the cafeteria. I saw her in the hall between classes and she said she was using lunchtimes to work on a research project in the library. But it was much too early in the year for anyone to be working on a research project. Had it not been for Brianna's presence, I might have thought Katherine and Dakota were just having another one of their tiffs. But during the previous fights, even the long one the spring before, no one had dared sit in Dakota's seat, the way Brianna now did.

Tuesday 10:58 A.M.

MY CELL PHONE vibrates. I flip it open and see the text: **Who this?**

Trembling again, I thumb the answer: **U no.**

She writes, **U have 2 turn urself in.**

No way.

Everyone looking 4 U. U cant hide 4ever.

Even as Dakota and I text back and forth, I'm starting to formulate a new plan. Maybe if I make her nervous enough, she'll try something dumb and desperate. Something that might make her reveal the truth about what happened. So I text back: **Bet?**

This time a reply doesn't come so quickly. Is she frantically plotting her next move?

The phone vibrates: **Where U @?**

As if I would tell her. But it makes me think. Going purely on gut instinct, I write: **Lets f2f.**

Again I wait, but not that long. She texts back: **Where?**

An unexpected chill envelops me. By asking where we

should meet, has Dakota just unknowingly confessed her guilt? Would *anyone* ever agree to meet someone they thought was a killer? No, of course not. So if Dakota is willing to meet me, it means one of two things: Either she doesn't believe I'm the killer, because she knows who the killer *really* is—her. Or she will bring the police. In either case, do I really want to go through with this?

I'm in the middle of trying to figure out the answer when the phone vibrates again. Thinking it's another text from Dakota, I flip it open. But it's not a text; it's a call from "unknown." I nervously lift the phone to my ear. "Hello?"

"Callie?" It's a male voice.

"Yes?"

"Hey, it's Jerry."

"Oh, hi!" That's a relief. For a moment I thought maybe it was Dakota purposefully calling from a different phone so I wouldn't think it was her.

"So listen, I just wanted to see how the phone's been working," he says.

"It's working fine, Jerry. Thanks for checking. And thanks again so much for helping me."

"No prob. So, uh . . . you okay? Need anything?"

I'm just about to tell him that I'm as well as can be expected when I realize that's not true. "Actually, there is something I need. I'm out of money and I'm scared that if I use my ATM card, I'll give the police another way to track me. I hate asking you, but could you lend me some? I promise I'll pay you back."

Jerry laughs. "Are you kidding? Of course. You want to meet somewhere?"

I almost agree when I catch myself. Jerry leave his house? Why would he risk being caught helping me? Isn't it strange how a few moments ago Dakota agreed to meet me and now Jerry calls and agrees to do the same thing? The third of Slade's three *P*s pops into my head—paranoia. "I'm not sure that's a good idea, Jerry. If anyone sees you with me, or we get caught, you could get into really big trouble. I think it would be a lot smarter if you just leave the money for me somewhere and I come and get it."

There's a pause. Then Jerry says, "Uh, well, uh, hey, listen, can I call you right back?"

"Okay . . ."

He's off the line and now I can't help feeling even more paranoid. What just happened seems odd. Like he had to check with someone else before answering me.

When the phone rings a few moments later, I almost don't answer. Then I do. "Hey, okay," Jerry says. "I got an idea. You know the warming room at the train station? There's an old bookcase there. People leave books after they finish them. I'll leave the money for you this afternoon in the last book on the first shelf, okay?"

I would feel grateful to him were it not for my suspicion that something isn't right. Still, I know I have to pretend. "Thank you, Jerry. You're such a sweetheart. I don't know what I'd do without you."

"Hey, no prob. So I'll probably get over to the station around three. You can pick it up anytime after that. But I wouldn't wait too long, you know? Someone might come by looking for a book to read and get a big surprise."

I pretend to laugh at the thought of someone picking up a used book and finding money inside.

"In fact, do me a favor, okay?" he goes on. "Send me a text after you get it. Just so I know?"

I tell him I will.

"Promise?"

"Yes, Jerry, I promise. And really, thanks so much." I close the cell phone. The more I think about it, the stranger it all seems. Jerry leave his cave voluntarily? He's going to touch a used book that who knows how many germy hands have held? No way. Not in this lifetime.

And now I realize something else. Dakota asked where I wanted to meet and I didn't answer. She hasn't followed up. Or has she, by getting Jerry involved?

Two nights after school began, my phone rang. The number came up as private. After staring uncertainly at it for a moment, I decided to answer.

"Hi." It was Dakota.

"Oh, hi," I said, surprised.

"So what's up?" she asked.

"Oh, well, nothing, except, you know, everything," I said. "I mean, how come you're not sitting with us anymore?"

"What does Katherine say?" she asked.

"You know her. She never says anything."

"Has anyone asked her?"

"Not when I was around."

"What do they say when she's not around?"

It never ceased to amaze me how certain she and Katherine were that everyone talked about them. "Everyone's just wondering what happened."

"And you're sure Katherine hasn't said anything?"

"Not to me."

There was a short pause and then she said, "Have you spoken to Slade?"

It didn't feel like we were having a conversation. Rather, it felt like she was running down a prepared list of questions.

"No," I answered.

There was another short silence, then that brief blank sound when another call is coming in. "It's my mom," Dakota said. "Talk to you later."

"Do you think I'm sexy?"

"Sure."

"You're going to do what I want you to do?"

"I said I would, and I will."

"Good, because I did what I said I'd do."

Tuesday 4:32 P.M.

A HUNDRED YARDS south of the train station, a bridge goes over the railroad tracks. That afternoon around four thirty, I ride toward the bridge on Alyssa Lamont's old pink bicycle. I have the lollipop in my mouth and I'm wearing the candy-cane framed glasses and pink baseball cap. I stop on the sidewalk at the middle of the bridge and look toward the station. On both sides of the tracks are long flat platforms. On the platform on the left side is the glass-enclosed warming room.

People stand on both platforms—nannies, laborers, men and women in business clothes with briefcases, and teenagers with backpacks filled with books. A southbound train pulls into the station. People get on and off, and a few moments later, the train leaves. But strangely, two men, one at either end of the platform, don't get on the train, nor are they now exiting the platform. They just stand there as if they're waiting for another train. One reads a folded newspaper. The other appears to be fiddling with an iPod.

A few minutes later, the same thing happens on the north-bound platform. A train pulls in, people get on and off. But when the train departs, there's still a woman on the far end of the platform and a man on the near end.

I wait and watch. It is nearly rush hour and not long before more trains come and go and more people get on and off. But those four people remain.

There was another change at the table. Katherine turned cool to me. Once again I felt like I was out of the loop. I felt confused and uncertain of what to do. But this time I wasn't as eager to find out why she was acting that way. I was still bothered by and unsure about what had happened at the party the night before school had begun.

Mia still came to the table at lunch, but she no longer asked whether anyone had plans or wanted to do something with her after school. She would just sit there quietly, trying to act like she didn't care.

Most of the girls at our table ate salads or brought yogurt and fruit or vegetables from home. Everyone agreed the school food was gross. The exception was Mia, who bought a school lunch each day and clearly enjoyed pasta and pizza and fries, as well as ice cream, pudding, or cake for dessert. One day at lunch, I noticed that Katherine had a frown on her face. She was staring at Mia, who, somewhat obliviously, was sliding her finger around the inside of a plastic container, collecting the very last traces of chocolate pudding, then sticking her finger in her mouth and licking it clean.

When Mia got up to return her tray to the kitchen, Katherine immediately turned to me. "Tell that fat pig that she's no longer sitting at this table."

The cheerful mood around the table vanished. Everyone went silent. Mia might not have been skinny, but she hardly qualified as fat. "Why?" I asked.

"Because she's disgusting and the way she eats is gross."

It was an order, and I knew I had a choice. Follow it, and remain at the table, or disobey, and be cut loose.

I watch from the bridge over the tracks while those four people below stand around not taking trains. Strangely, instead of feeling angry at Jerry, I feel bad. When my phone suddenly became untraceable, did the police figure out that I'd gone to his house and that he'd helped me? I wouldn't be surprised if they threatened to arrest him if he didn't cooperate.

But what if I'm wrong? Those four people could be standing on those platforms for a hundred reasons that have nothing to do with me. But how can I know for certain? I have an idea and take out my cell phone and, as promised, send Jerry a text: **Got the $$. Thx!**

Down on the platforms nothing happens. I wait and watch. One of the men is still reading the paper. The woman appears to be thumbing a BlackBerry. So it looks like I was wrong and there *is* such a thing as being too paranoid. I decide to ride over to the bike rack. From there I'll take the stairs down to the warming room and get the money.

Then, all at once, the people on the platforms press their

fingers against their right ears. It looks very strange until I realize what it means. They're all wearing earpieces.

The next thing I know, they're jogging quickly down the platforms. They must be headed for the warming room. The two on the northbound side will probably take the walkway under the tracks to get there.

But that's not what happens. The two people on the south-bound platform jog right past the warming room. The two on the northbound platform pass the entrance to the walkway.

And that's when I realize they're headed for the bridge . . . and me.

Tuesday 4:39 P.M.

I QUICKLY LOOK around. Traffic passes behind me on the bridge. There's the heavy low grumble of a diesel engine as a garbage truck approaches. In the meantime I can hear slapping footsteps coming up the steps from the platform.

The garbage truck is passing. It has one of those big scoop-shaped bins at the rear.

I toss the cell phone into it.

A moment later, the first earpiece man reaches the bridge, breathing hard, his right hand still pressed against his ear.

He looks around, then stares right at me!

I feel myself freeze, my hands gripping the handles of the bike so hard my knuckles turn white, my heart racing.

There's a loud screech as a police car flies around the corner and starts to speed up the bridge in our direction. At the same time, the earpiece man starts to run toward me.

Something heavy sinks inside me. Even with this bike, there's no way I can get away from them. This is it. It's all over. I'm caught.

* * *

The night after Katherine ordered me to tell Mia she couldn't sit with us any longer, Dakota called.

"I heard what happened at lunch today," she said.

"Uh-huh." I didn't know what else to do except acknowledge what she'd said and wonder why she was calling me.

"You know it's all about power. She's the most evil, nasty, insecure person ever. She has to constantly reassure herself that she's in control, and the only way she can do that is by making people do things for her that they don't want to do. You think it's any surprise that she chose *you* to tell Mia not to sit with us anymore? No way. She chose you because she knew you'd have the hardest time doing it."

I listened silently.

"And you know why you'll do it?" Dakota asked in a condescending tone.

"No," I said, almost befuddled by the meanness I felt emanating from her. We might have shared a common frenemy, but that clearly did not make us friends.

"Look at what she's already gotten you to give up," Dakota said. "You'll do it because you have nothing left to lose."

chapter 33

Tuesday 4:41 P.M.

WHEN THE POLICE car races past me, I spin around and realize why: it's chasing the garbage truck.

Only the officer inside the car doesn't know he's chasing the truck. He's just following the signal from my cell phone, which appears to be going in the same direction.

But that still leaves the man with the earpiece, who is twenty feet away, running straight for me. I tense and brace myself.

He runs right past . . . in the same direction the police car was going.

Feeling like I ducked a bullet aimed straight for my head, I will my body to relax, but my heart is still pounding. Trembling, hoping I can keep my balance, I get on the pink bike and begin riding in the opposite direction. I need to get away from the bridge as fast as possible, before that police car catches up to the garbage truck and they figure out what I did.

Only I have no idea where I'm going.

Moments later I'm riding down the sidewalk through

town, passing stores and nannies pushing small children in strollers. It feels strange to ride around disguised as a young girl, stranger still that the disguise is actually working. It's like some kind of weird out-of-body experience. As if I've done such a good job of disguising myself that I'm not Callie anymore. But what good is it doing? The police are still looking for me. I've thrown away my phone and have no way of communicating with anyone. I have no money for food and no place left to hide, and I'm still no closer to proving who really killed Katherine.

So maybe there's no point in trying to hide. The official opening of the new town center is scheduled for tomorrow. I know that Slade and the rest of the crew will be working hard today to get everything ready. Maybe my only chance now is to get closer.

When I get there, the landscapers are planting shrubs and rolling out thick green sod to create a perfect lawn. Plumbers, electricians, and carpenters stream in and out while a group of firemen uses one of the ladder trucks to hang celebratory red, white, and blue banners over the truck bays.

I ride the pink bike around to the back, where vans and cars are parked in the new lot. There's Slade's pickup. The tarry scent of fresh asphalt in my nose, I leave the bike on the edge of the lot, then wait until no one is looking and scramble into the truck. Slade's pickup has an extended cab, which means there's a narrow row of seats in the back. It's supposed to be large enough to carry passengers but there's barely enough legroom for anyone taller than five feet, which makes it a perfect place to hide.

I slide into the backseat and look around. Something's different and it's not just the green-and-gold Fort Benning, Georgia, parking sticker. It's the odor of stale cigarette smoke.

But now my attention is drawn to something else. Through the windshield I see the back door to the town center open, and Mia and her father come out, accompanied by a prim blonde woman wearing a dark suit and carrying a briefcase. I'll bet anything she's a lawyer.

Does Mia have more to do with this than I know? More than she's told me?

More people come out. Oh my God! It's Griffen and two men in dark suits. Is one his father and the other—the one with the thick brown leather satchel—a lawyer? They all stop in the parking lot and talk in a relaxed manner that makes it appear as if they're familiar with each other. As the conversation continues, Griffen steps close to Mia and slides his arm around her waist.

They know each other? Well enough for him to put his arm around her? It's mind boggling. How is this possible?

Hidden by the tall front seats and the darkly tinted rear windows in the pickup, I have to wonder. Is Griffen the reason Mia's attitude toward Katherine has changed recently? Was he what she was referring to when she said there was life outside Soundview High? One thing's for certain. They both had excellent reasons to despise Katherine.

And, it was Mia who insisted I come to the kegger.

And Mia who wrote, **Dont U just want 2 kill her sometimes?**

169

I could be wrong about Dakota.

The group splits up and gets into cars.

I lie down on the backseat, ball up an old sweatshirt, and lay my head on it, breathing in Slade's scent, missing him so much it hurts, trying to figure out what Mia and Griffen could have to do with Katherine's murder. On the floor behind the front seat are Slade's red-and-white cooler and a couple of empty coffee containers from Dunkin' Donuts. There's something under the front seat and I reach down to pull it out for a better look.

It's a pair of panty hose, and the thought of why it's here makes my stomach twist. There's only one reason and I wish I didn't know what it was. But what did I expect? That after I broke up with him, he'd swear an oath of celibacy?

But it could explain some things. If there's another girl . . . If he's caught between her and me . . . Was that why he wanted to speak to me face-to-face this morning? Did he want to tell me that he had made up his mind? But the photo taped to his computer was of him and me, not him and her.

It's one more thing that will drive me crazy. But there's nothing I can do except ask Slade when I see him. So I lie there, trying not to think about the panty hose or what they imply. Or Mia and Griffen, or what their coming out of the police station together means. The rear seat is considerably more comfortable than the floor of the tree house, and I snuggle against the balled-up sweatshirt, feeling the fog of fatigue gradually thicken.

* * *

You'll do it because you have nothing left to lose. In an awful way, Dakota was right. I'd given up Slade to be in the IC. Now the IC was all I had.

But to stay in the IC, I had to tell Mia she could no longer sit at our table. That meant I'd have to accept my role as Katherine's gofer . . . for as long as she wanted.

Was that who I wanted to be?

Tuesday 5:42 P.M.

I'M HOLDING MY breath underwater. Something pokes gently at my arm, and I slowly glide up to the surface to see what it is. I splash into consciousness and blink. It's dark. I'm lying on the backseat of a car. . . . Wait, now I remember. . . . It's Slade's truck. A shadowy face tilts over the front seat, looking down at me.

"Uh, excuse me," he begins before I turn fully toward him, "but what—" In the shock of recognition, he catches himself. "Cal!" His voice rises and I sleepily press my finger to my lips. He twists his head around as if looking through the windows to make sure no one heard him, then whispers harshly, "Are you crazy?"

"I need your help."

"For God's sake!" He looks around again, then back at me as if he can't believe what he's seeing.

"Please, Slade." I start to sit up.

"Stay down!"

I do as he says. I wish he were happy to see me instead of irate.

"Slade, I know you're still upset—"

"You don't know anything!"

"Does it have something to do with this?" I lift the panty hose up to his eye level.

He twitches with surprise, then frowns. "Where'd you find that?"

"On the floor back here. Is this what you wanted to tell me about this morning?"

The frown becomes a scowl. "What are you talking about?"

"That there's someone else?"

His eyes leave mine. "That's not what I wanted to tell you."

"Are you sure?"

"I think I'd know," he answers. Now his forehead bunches. "Is that Alyssa's sweatshirt?"

I nod.

"How'd you . . . ?" he begins, then realizes the answer. "You went into my house?"

"I was hungry and dirty and needed a new disguise."

He shakes his head. "You are a piece of work, Cal."

"Please don't be angry," I whisper, nearly begging.

That seems to take the anger away. Slade leans his forehead against the headrest. I stay low in the backseat and wonder what he's thinking. I wonder what *I'm* thinking. Nothing, really. I'm just here for now, happy to be with him, to feel connected to him.

Not knowing what else to say, I ask, "How's the preparation going?"

He raises his eyes over the headrest. "Well enough to fake it. Congresswoman Jenkins will come and make a speech. They'll take pictures and video for the news. As soon as the crowd leaves, we'll come back in and finish the job."

I forgot that Dakota's mother is going to preside over the official opening tomorrow morning. She'll be right here, in the town center. . . .

I have a crazy, desperate idea.

"I have to see her."

"Who?"

"Dakota's mom."

Slade stares at me. "You really are out of your mind."

"Yes. Next question?"

"Seriously, Shrimp, it ain't happening."

But the more I think about it, the more certain I am that it's probably my last chance. If I can sow a seed of doubt in Congresswoman Jenkins's mind . . . "It could happen . . . if you'll help me."

"Sorry. No way."

"Why not?"

Slade sighs with frustration and runs his fingers through his hair. He doesn't seem to have a reason, other than, like me, he must realize how crazy and risky it is.

"What if it's the only way I can prove I'm innocent?" I ask.

He turns away and gazes out the window. Why should he risk being arrested for me? True, he's already helped me, but I'm the only person who knows that and I swore I'd never tell. And I never, will. Not after what I've already done to him.

But I can't do this alone. I have to convince him to help me. "If I can get Griffen Clemment to testify that Dakota sent him death threats that mentioned killing Katherine, then all I have to do is get Congresswoman Jenkins to check the knives in her kitchen. And if she does that, she's going to find that one of the knives is missing. Because it's in police custody as evidence."

Slade looks at me and raises an eyebrow. "You think Dakota would be stupid enough to take a knife from her own kitchen and use it to kill Katherine? As if no one would think to check?"

"I—I'm just saying it's possible," I stammer meekly. "I mean, I saw the knife. It was the same brand."

He snorts derisively. Instead of me convincing him, he's making me doubt. But there's still so much I don't know. And I can't think of anything else to do. "It's my only chance," I whisper. "You may be right, but if I don't try this, I'm going to go to jail for a crime I didn't commit. Is that what you want?"

Silence.

Two days passed and I didn't tell Mia she couldn't sit at the table. She sat with us, and Katherine pretended like nothing was wrong. But I knew that she wouldn't forget.

On the third day, I went into the cafeteria and Katherine and the other girls weren't sitting at the regular table. They were at a smaller round table. There was room for six and all the seats were taken. It was Zelda's beach house all over again. Katherine was shutting me out until I did what she wanted me to.

Only this time I knew something I hadn't known the last time. Even if I did what she wanted, it wouldn't end. There'd be more distasteful tasks. Why? Because I served no other purpose for her. She kept Jodie around because Jodie appeared in ads and was a school celebrity. She had Zelda because she was rich, and Kirsten because her mother provided access to cool things to do in the city. She had Brianna because Brianna was her new project, much the way I had once been a project. And why had she kept Dakota?

Maybe she was thinking like the Chinese general who said, "Keep your friends close, and your enemies closer."

I sat down at a lunch table by myself, not surprised to be shut out but feeling stung just the same. Someone sat down near me with a tray, but I didn't focus on her until she asked, "What's going on?" It was Mia.

"It's obvious, isn't it?"

"But why?"

There was no point in telling her why. It would only make her feel bad. So I said, "I don't know."

Mia bit into a cheeseburger and chewed rhythmically, her eyes downcast. As bad as I felt for myself, I felt equally bad for her. She'd done nothing wrong. All she wanted was to be in that crowd. The more I thought about how unfair it was, the angrier I got. Only I wasn't sure who I was angrier at—Katherine for being so cruel, or myself for being so stupid.

Mia swallowed, then said, "You know why she dumps on us?"

I shrugged and shook my head.

"What's the one thing all those girls have in common?" Mia asked.

I glanced over at the table. "I don't know, what?"

"Money," Mia said. "Lots of it."

I thought about that for a moment. "Not Katherine."

"Are you kidding?"

"Her dad doesn't have a job," I said.

Mia leaned close. "She's a *Remington*. Her dad doesn't *need* a job. Her mom comes from, like, a totally wealthy family. That's why we're not at that table, because our families don't have as much money as theirs." Her cheeks bulging with food, she shook her head. "God, I hate her."

Deep down, I didn't agree. It was hard to imagine that it was really about money, but maybe that was the easiest way for Mia to rationalize it.

"What's so great about Katherine, anyway?" Mia asked. "So what if she has rich friends and a snobby attitude? I don't need her friends and I don't need her. I can have my own table and my own friends. How about it, Callie? Want to sit at my table?"

Why not? I thought. I had nowhere else to sit.

"SLADE," I IMPLORE him in a whisper from the backseat of the pickup. *"Please?"*

He still doesn't answer. He's turned away and is facing the front. All I see is the back of his head.

"Don't you care?"

He grips the steering wheel and leans forward, resting his forehead on the back of his hands. "Don't I care? For God's sake, Cal, did you forget that you're the one who broke up with me? Did you ever stop to think about what you did? You just plain straight up wrecked me. And now . . . now you want me to help you?"

We sit in silence. So I guess the picture on his computer means less than I thought. And he still hasn't explained the panty hose. Maybe I should just open the door and get out. But I can't give up. I just can't! "Okay, Slade, you're right. I'm not in a position to ask you to do anything. Just tell me one thing. What time is Congresswoman Jenkins scheduled to speak tomorrow?"

He sighs loudly and shakes his head as if he thinks I've lost my mind, but he also digs into his back pocket, comes up with a piece of paper, and holds it close to the window and near his face, trying to read it in the dim light. "She's supposed to arrive at ten and take a tour of the facility. The ceremony starts at eleven. She leaves right after."

"There has to be some time in there," I tell him. "After the tour and before the ceremony. She's going to want to primp before she goes in front of the cameras."

He twists around and looks over the seat at me. "And what do you think you're going to do? Just stroll in the front door and have a chat?"

I can't answer. I don't know what I'm going to do. I only know that I've got all night to come up with a plan. "I'll think of something." I expect him to turn away, but he doesn't. He stays there, twisted in his seat, looking at me.

"I'm sorry, Slade. I really am. And . . . I know you don't want to hear this, but I really do still love you, no matter what happens."

He lowers his head and stares down. I can't believe what an idiot I was. Here is the one real, true thing in my life and I threw it away. How pathetic. And yet . . . and yet . . . there's still a little time. There's still tonight. Maybe there's a chance. I reach out and touch his hair, run my fingers gently over his cheek.

This time, he doesn't yell. He raises his face. Is it my imagination or are his eyes glistening? He reaches around the seat toward me and I feel his fingers touch my cheek. He slides his knuckles along my jaw and toward my lips and I kiss his fingers. Maybe it's insane to feel happy in a situation like this, but

I do. I'm so glad to be with him again . . . to feel his caring again. The seat stops him from coming closer to me, but it doesn't keep me from stretching up toward him. Closer . . . closer . . . until at last our lips meet.

We kiss in that awkward position. The dampness I feel where our cheeks meet must be from tears. His tears.

"I made a mistake," I whisper. "Crazy things happen. Things you never expect. You look back and can't believe what you did. Like it couldn't have been you."

"I know," he whispers, kissing my face and lips. "I know."

"And . . . you forgive me?"

"Sure, Shrimp. I forgive you."

"And the panty hose in your truck?"

"Some clients want a texture in the plaster so we rub it with old panty hose."

That's a relief! "And . . . you still love me?"

He's quiet for a moment. Then he sniffs. "I'll always love you."

He tells me to lie low in the truck and wait. After the last worker leaves, he'll come get me. I fall asleep trying to figure out what I can say to Congresswoman Jenkins tomorrow.

When I wake up, it's dark and very quiet. I'm instantly alert. Something isn't right. Raising my head, I look through the windshield of the pickup. The parking lot is empty.

Then, near the back of the town center, I see something glow red in the dark—the ember of a cigarette.

I let myself out of the pickup. The air is cool and chilly and I hug myself to stay warm. Slade is sitting in the shadows, smoking, with a half-finished bottle on the ground beside him.

"Everyone's gone. Why didn't you come get me?"

Instead of answering, he takes a drag of his cigarette and exhales a plume into the air. "Know what I was just thinking about?"

"How could I?"

"How unfair it was that your birthday came right in the middle of those two months when I wasn't allowed to speak or write to you." He looks up with a crooked smile on his face. "Happy birthday, Shrimp."

"Thanks." I offer him my hands, to help him up. "Now come on. We've got things to do."

He studies my hands, then shakes his head as if he can't believe that someone as little as me really thinks she can help him up. But he takes hold just the same.

Limping slightly, he leads me across the dark, empty parking lot, around the orange cones blocking the newly painted white lines of parking spaces, through the back door of the new town center. In the hallway, under a bare yellowish lightbulb, he stops and looks back at me. His eyes are sad.

"What?" I ask.

Instead of answering, he gives me half a smile and shakes his head again, then takes my hand and leads me up the concrete steps to the second floor.

He pushes through a door and we enter a large shadowy room illuminated by some streetlights outside. The smell of drying paint is in the air. As my eyes adjust to the dark, I can see that this is the new lounge. Or at least, it *will* be the new lounge once it's finished. Right now, the floor is still bare concrete. New rolls of carpet rest against a wall. In one corner couches covered with plastic sheets are positioned around a large flat-screen TV. In another corner is the ancient pool table from the old EMS building. Along the wall are cabinets and a sink, a stove, and a refrigerator, all with their new-appliance labels and warnings still attached.

I open one of the cabinet doors under the sink. The space will work. I turn and put my arms around Slade. "I wish we could just stay like this forever," I whisper, craning my neck up and feeling his lips against mine, his scratchy stubble against my face. "Stay with me?"

He hesitates, then says, "Wish I could, but I've got to get home and clean up for the ceremony." He gives me one last hug, then leans back and looks into the empty cabinet. "You *sure* this is what you want to do?"

"No, but I don't know what else to do."

Lunch was almost over and Mia and I took our trays to the kitchen. Turning back, we found Kirsten coming toward us, no doubt with a message from Katherine.

"Can I talk to you?" she said to Mia.

Mia's eyes darted toward the table where Katherine was sitting, then back to Kirsten. "Okay."

I watched the two girls walk off together and stand by the window. Kirsten crossed her arms and spoke. Mia's mouth fell open. Then, for a moment, it looked as if she would burst into tears. But her lips closed, her jaw became firm, her eyes narrowed, and she began to march toward Katherine's table.

At the table, Katherine had been leaning forward in conversation, but I knew she must have had one eye on what was happening between Kirsten and Mia. Now, with Mia storming toward her, Katherine sat up straight, and for the first time that I could remember, her face went pale.

Not certain exactly what Mia intended to do, I began to hurry toward the table. Mia, her red face filled with fury, stopped and hovered over Katherine, who was doing her best to stare straight back. Maybe it was only my imagination, but I would have sworn that inside, Katherine was quaking with fear.

"How dare you!" Mia shouted. At the shrill sound of her voice, the closer half of the cafeteria went silent. Heads turned and kids rose from their seats to see what was going on as Mia went off on a tirade. "It wasn't enough that you had to shut me out of your table, but you had to send one of your little robots over to make sure I knew the reason. Well, let me tell you something, Miss Prim-Proper Phony, you are going to get yours. Believe me. When I'm done with you, you'll wish you'd . . . you'd never been adopted!"

Katherine went white. Mia turned and marched out of the cafeteria. Behind her some kids began to cheer and whistle. It was impossible to tell whether they were expressing their personal feelings about Katherine or just voicing their approval of the entertaining nature of Mia's outburst.

I followed Mia into the hall and down to the girls' room. By the time I got there, she'd locked herself in a stall and I could hear her gasping for breath and sobbing. "You okay?" I asked.

"Yeah, I'm just . . . I think I kind of freaked myself out. . . ."

"You were fabulous!" I said, hoping to make her feel better. "I mean, no one's ever done that to her before . . . and in front of everyone!"

"Yeah . . . I just . . . I don't know . . . lost it. She is such an evil piece of slime."

"Well, she deserved it," I said. "So . . . I think I know what Kirsten said."

In the stall, Mia blew her nose. "How?"

"Because Katherine wanted me to tell you and I refused."

"Why?"

"Because it isn't true. And because I didn't want to hurt your feelings, and because I knew it would never end. Even if I did what she wanted, she'd just come up with something worse next time."

"God, I hate her," Mia muttered on the other side of the stall door. "I just so hate her."

"I'm not sure she's worth hating," I said.

I heard a rustling sound; then the stall door opened and Mia came out. Her eyes were red and her face was splotchy. She went to the mirror and started to fix her makeup. "You're *sure* I'm not a fat pig?"

I winced at the thought of Kirsten delivering that news back in the cafeteria. What a horrible thing to do.

"Not even close."

Mia looked at me in the mirror. "You mean it?"

"Yes. But what was that thing about Katherine being adopted?"

Mia stared down at a sink. "It was really a low blow. But I just couldn't come up with anything else that I knew would hurt."

"It's true?"

She nodded. "She told me once. I mean, a thousand years ago when we were, like, in third grade. Before she became Katherine the Terrible."

"But there are lots of adopted kids. Why would it hurt her?"

"I don't know," Mia said with a shrug. "That's just the way she is. Whatever problem she has with it is in her head. Not anyone else's."

The bell rang; it was time to go to class. "Well, I just want you to know you put on a world-class performance today," I said, and gave her a hug before heading for the door.

"Would you do something with me?" Mia suddenly asked. I stopped and looked at her.

"I want to write something for the school paper," she said. "Would you write it with me?"

"What's it about?" I asked.

"I'll call you tonight."

chapter 36

Wednesday 7:23 A.M.

IN THE DARK lounge, I rest on one of the plastic-covered couches, knowing I won't be able to fall asleep again. My thoughts are scattered. Will I ever get to sleep in my own bed again? What chance do I really have of convincing Congresswoman Jenkins that her own daughter killed Katherine? If Dakota did it, why did she pick me to blame? Was it just random? Was I simply the first one she came across at the kegger after she killed Katherine? Or was it planned? She had to know about the peer mediation. Did she think she had to act before Katherine and I had a chance to resolve our issues?

But what if I'm totally wrong and she had nothing to do with it? What if it was Mia and Griffen? Or someone else entirely? Slade said they'd even treated him like a possible suspect.

What if they really have no idea?

What if they just *hope* I'm the one?

Outside, the sky is brightening. I hear car doors banging and voices. The workers are here early to set up for the celebration.

I slide off the couch, scamper to the cabinet under the sink, and crawl inside.

Lying in the dark, with the cabinet door closed and the scents of new wood and plastic plumbing in my nose, I now have to wait. Hours pass. Finally, somewhere in the room, a door squeaks open and closes quietly. I remain still under the sink, feeling an almost feverish anxiety. Is it Slade? Or someone else? The cabinet door opens. Slade is squatting there, light flooding in around him. I squint. He's clean-shaven and wearing a navy blue crewneck. Only his bloodshot eyes give away his lack of sleep. His expression is grim. I wish he would look happy to see me.

"You okay?" he asks.

"Yes. You?"

"Tired." He glances around inside the cabinet. "You know this is never going to work, right?"

"Got a better idea?" I ask.

He shrugs. "Time to get ready. They're coming."

The cabinet door closes and I'm back in the dark. But now, I see the flaws in my plan that I couldn't see last night. The urge to crawl out and run surges through me. But it's too late. The building is filling with workers. If I try to sneak out now, I'm bound to be seen.

Seconds pass. Now instead of feeling eager to continue, I'm dreading it. I'm trapped at ground zero, right above the police department. What was I thinking by coming here?

A door opens. I hear people enter the lounge.

A man's voice: "As you can see, this will be the new lounge. By having the emergency services and fire department share one space, we'll realize a pretty significant energy savings."

A woman's voice: "Good idea."

The man's voice: "Well, that's about it for the tour."

The woman: "Thank you. It's been wonderful. You've done a very good job."

A door opens and closes.

The woman: "How much time?"

A different man's voice: "About five minutes. Looks like there's about a hundred people out there."

"Channel Twelve?" the woman asks.

"No, but Simmons from the *Journal* with a photographer. And that new girl from the *Shoreline Express*."

The woman replies, "All right, I'm just going to freshen up and review some notes. I'll be right down."

A door opens and closes. The lounge becomes quiet. Is it possible that Congresswoman Jenkins is here alone? That this little part of my plan has actually worked? My heart is thudding, and despite the coolness around me, my skin feels warm and moist. I'm scared about what's going to happen next. I press my fingers against the inside of the cabinet door and a crack of light peeks in. I can't see Dakota's mom. I'm starting to push the door farther when I hear what sounds like her speaking on a phone: "Yes, half an hour at the most. Right. What did Salinger say about the spending cuts? Good, good. Well, we'll just have to see if they get enough votes. What? I know, it's hard to believe that they haven't found her yet. The whole police force looking for one kid and they can't figure out where she is. What can I say? He's my brother. I know it looks bad. Well, hopefully they'll find her soon and put an end to it. Uh-huh. Yes. I'll speak to you later."

The phone snaps shut. The lounge is quiet. It's now or never. Blood pounding in my ears, I push open the cabinet door and crawl out. Congresswoman Jenkins is standing near the window with an open compact, taking advantage of the sunlight to touch up her makeup.

"Excuse me?"

Startled, she jerks her head up from the compact, then frowns when she sees me. Her eyes dart to the door, as if she doesn't understand how I got in here without her noticing. "Yes?"

She has no idea who I am. To her I'm just some little kid dressed in pink and white who's magically appeared out of nowhere.

"I have to talk to you about Katherine Remington-Day," I begin.

Her eyes widen with surprise, then narrow as if to focus more clearly. "You're . . . the Carson girl?"

I nod and her eyes again go to the door. Is she considering whether to dash through it? Call for help?

"Please," I beg her. "The night Katherine was killed, Dakota knew about it before anyone else. She told me where to look for the body. If you go home today and check your knives, you're going to find that you're missing the one that matches the description of the murder weapon."

Congresswoman Jenkins stares at me. It must be a lot to take in all at once. "You're saying . . . that *my daughter* Dakota killed Katherine? With a knife from my kitchen?"

With a slow nod I reply, "I don't expect you to believe me.

No mother would. But I have to ask you to consider what I'm saying. I bet you had no idea that she sent death threats about Katherine."

Dakota's mother's eyebrows sink into a **V**. I expect the next thing she says to be that she doesn't believe me. Instead, she asks, "How do you know about that?"

This catches me completely off guard. She *knows* about the death threats? "Griffen Clemment told me. He's the one Dakota—"

"I know who he is." She cuts me short, then stares at me again, as if trying to decide what to do next. "What do you want from me?" she finally asks.

"I want you to consider the possibility that what I'm saying might be true. That the police are looking for the wrong suspect. That this whole thing is a huge mistake."

"Why can't you tell them yourself?"

"They'll never believe me. All the evidence makes it look like I did it."

"Yes, everyone's aware of that." Her voice hardens. She's moved past astonishment. Her protective instincts have kicked into gear. "Did Slade Lamont tell you to do this?"

All I can do is shake my head. I can't think of anything to say. How can she know about Slade? How much more is there that I don't know?

She purses her lips and nods slowly, as if my silence is affirmation. "Whatever you have to say, you can say to the police . . . *yourself.*" Her voice becomes stern and cold. She walks across the room, opens the door, and leaves.

I run to the closest window and yank it open, then hurry to the old pool table. After Slade said good-bye this morning, he left the end ajar. Now I wiggle in feetfirst and swing the end closed, sealing myself inside like a trapdoor spider.

It's dark except for the light that comes down through the pockets. Lying flat and straight, I barely have room to fit under the gullies.

I still can't understand how Dakota's mom could know about Slade.

But there's nothing I can do now except wait.

DOES MONEY MAKE YOU POPULAR?

by Callie Carson

For as long as there's been high school, students have wondered what makes kids popular. Some people say the standard for popularity changes from generation to generation. Is having money the standard for our generation?

It's the age-old question: what does one have to do to be popular? After grades, it could be the biggest concern some students have. And in some cases, it may be even more important than grades.

There was a time when it was easy to know who was popular and who wasn't. If you were a jock or a cheerleader, you were popular. Then it changed. Sometimes it seemed like the coolest and most popular kids were the ones with their own bands. Or the artists. Or the kids in student government. Or even the brainiac geeks, with their super-high GPAs and science awards.

But lately a new group seems to dominate. They may have talent, or none at all. They might be pretty, or get good grades, or not. What's the one thing they do have? Money. Enough to spend whatever they want on clothes and entertainment and other kinds of fun, and never even have to think about it.

The strange thing is, with one or two exceptions, these kids didn't earn a penny of it themselves. For the most part they've never had to work a day in their lives. It's not like in the old days, when kids had to be good at something to be popular. Back then, athletes and cheerleaders had to train. Musicians had to rehearse. Student government kids had to campaign and run for election. Geeks had to study.

These days, it seems, all you have to do is be born rich.

chapter 37

Wednesday 11:02 A.M.

SILENCE. I LIE in my new hiding place in the pool table, feeling worried and scared and baffled. Then comes a rumble of commotion and voices in the hall. A door bangs open and I hear heavy footsteps and breathing as several people rush into the room.

"Check everywhere," a man orders. "The closets, cabinets, everything."

I hear shuffling, banging, and the scraping of furniture being moved. "She's not here, sir."

"The window," someone says.

"Damn it!" another man grunts, as if angry with himself that he didn't notice it sooner.

"You think she went down the fire escape?"

"Down, or up. One of you go each way."

More grunts. I imagine two police officers climbing out the window to the fire escape. A walkie-talkie crackles on. A man in the room asks, "Any sign of her?"

"Negative," comes the reply over the walkie-talkie.

"McGregor and Petersen, you in the front?" asks the man.

"Yes, sir."

"I want one of you on either side of that crowd. Watch for her."

"Ten-four, sir."

I listen as he gives more orders and suddenly realize something I didn't think of before. Because of the ceremony, the whole police department is probably here. For the moment no one's out on patrol, no one's taking the day off. I couldn't be more surrounded.

"Wilson," the man in the room says, "anything on the roof?"

"Negative, sir."

"Palluci?"

"Yes, sir?"

"Go out in the front with McGregor and Petersen. Keep your eyes on that crowd. When people start to leave after the congresswoman's speech, look for anything she could hide in. You see a baby stroller, check it."

"Ten-four."

Another voice in the lounge says, "Heating ducts?"

"Christ, only in the movies," mutters the man giving orders, who I think must be Chief Jenkins.

"Ready to stake your job on that?" asks the other man.

"Wilson, go find a janitor or someone who knows where the ducts are and check them."

"Ten-four, sir."

A door opens and closes. Is the police chief still here? Is he alone in the lounge or did he leave, too? I strain to hear what's going on. Then there's a burst of walkie-talkie static. "Chief?"

"Whatcha got, Howard?"

"Nothing, sir."

"You checked *under* the cars, too?"

"Affirmative, sir."

"Okay. Remain where you are and keep your eyes open. She can't have just disappeared."

"Ten-four."

The lounge goes quiet, but I can hear breathing. I'm pretty sure Police Chief Jenkins is still here, but there could be someone else, as well. I wait. How long is he going to stay in the lounge? Why doesn't he leave? I hear a faint hiss and a thump, as if a window was just closed. "She's got to be somewhere in this building," he says.

"Or she could be hiding in that crowd," the other man answers in a way that makes me think he's an equal or a confidant. He didn't feel the need to add "sir" or "chief."

"It's only a hundred people," Chief Jenkins replies.

"Someone could be helping her."

It's quiet for a moment. Then the police chief mumbles, "Christ, what a mess."

"Did you ask her about the medical review board?" the other man asks.

"She won't talk about it," Chief Jenkins answers.

"What about the other girl and the Clemment kid?"

I lie perfectly still, afraid to move, trying desperately to hear an answer. The "Clemment kid" has to be Griffen. What could he possibly have to do with this? But just as the police chief begins to answer, his words are drowned out by applause coming from outside. The next thing I clearly hear is the other man saying, "The congresswoman's leaving?"

"That was quick." Chief Jenkins must be standing beside the window, looking down at the crowd.

"And still no sign of her," the other man says gravely and without the astonishment I'd expect to accompany that statement. "What do you make of it, Sam?"

"Damned if I know."

"Know what worries me?" the other man says. "That we may *never* know."

Know what? I wonder. What are they talking about? Are they worried they may never know who did it? Why did the other man bring up the medical review board? Was Mia the "other girl" they were talking about? And what is Griffen Clemment's role in this? I wish Chief Jenkins would answer, but there's only more silence until the other man says, "I better get moving." I hear something faint that might be a soft pat on the shoulder. "I'm sorry, Sam."

The opinion piece in the Soundview High School *Bugle* was supposed to have had both Mia's and my names on it. That was what she said would happen. But there it was with only my name on it, causing a big stir. Even I was surprised when I reread it. Somehow it looked and sounded different on my computer than it did in black-and-white print on the opinion page. At school some kids came up and congratulated me, but it seemed they were impressed more by my bravery than by what I'd had to say. Others glanced in my direction, frowned, and shook their heads, as if I'd voluntarily climbed into the lion's cage.

As soon as first period was over, I looked for Mia in the hall and the girls' room but couldn't find her. I did the same thing after second period. By the end of third, I was almost certain she was avoiding me, so I sent a text: **Have 2 talk 2 U.**

The reply came almost instantly: **Home sick.**

So not only had Mia left my name alone on the piece we'd cowritten; she'd left me alone in school to face the reaction. I couldn't help wondering just how sick she was.

chapter 38

Wednesday 2:55 P.M.

HIDING IN THE cabinet under the sink was uncomfortable, but being crammed into the pool table is way worse. I'm afraid any movement I make will result in a noise, and there's no place to move anyway. It's hard staying in one endless position with various parts of my body pressing against the wood until they throb painfully, then seem to go numb, then awaken and throb again. Quietly, I make whatever tiny adjustments I can, trying to take the pressure off the points that hurt the most.

Meanwhile, it feels like hours have passed, but I know that's just what I imagine, and it probably hasn't been nearly that long. What keeps me going and helps me endure this confinement is a sort of astonished hope. So far, my plan has worked! I'm not sure I really believed that it would. But I got to Congresswoman Jenkins and didn't get caught. And I have to believe that no matter how much she loves her daughter, no matter how much she doesn't want to believe a thing I've said, I've sowed a seed of doubt. Somewhere in her mind, she's got to be wondering. At the very least, when she goes into her kitchen tonight, won't she have to check her knives?

But now that feels like the easy part, compared to what I have to do next. The plan I've set for myself requires me to stay in the pool table until after everyone's gone, when I'll emerge and sneak out of the town center. But it's hard to wait in this painful position, especially when I'm not tired and can't count on a nap to help me pass the hours. But it's like everything else I've done. I'll just have to force myself to make it to the end.

And the time does pass. I can tell by the subtle, barely noticeable changes in the light coming through the pockets of the table. Especially when it begins to fade and then, finally, go dark.

Yet I still don't move. Instead, I listen—for the sounds of doors closing, of voices bidding each other good night, of car engines starting.

And then, after another eon, I feel like it's time. I've been in here so long that my body is beyond stiff. My joints are frozen. But it worked! A whole police force couldn't find me!

I'm so eager to get out that I push a little too hard on the end of the pool table and it swings open. *Thunk!* It bumps against the wall. Instantly, I freeze and listen for someone somewhere in the building to ask, "What was that?" But there's no sound. It's been a long day and the ceremony is over and I'm sure they've all gone.

Carefully, I inch my way out of the pool table until the tips of my fingers touch the floor, and I ease myself the rest of the way out like a butterfly crawling out of its chrysalis. The next thing I know, I'm crouching low, finding it hard to believe how good it feels to be out of that tiny cramped hiding place. The first thing I notice is that the room is not quite dark. I've misjudged. But at least the light is gray and I can see that it's twilight outside. That's not bad. All I have to do now is wait quietly here in the lounge until it's dark, and then go.

For a long moment I stay crouched, my feet and fingertips on the cool concrete floor, and take deep breaths to steady myself before moving again.

Finally I feel like I'm ready to stand. I lean back on my haunches and slowly rise.

And find myself staring at a man sitting on one of the plastic-covered couches.

"I couldn't do it," Mia said that night when I called to ask why she'd taken her name off the article in the *Bugle*. "I just didn't want it to look like it was some kind of personal vendetta."

"So now it looks like it was *my* personal vendetta," I said bitterly. "Thanks a lot."

"No, everyone knows what happened in the cafeteria. Even if my name wasn't on that article, they know how I feel about her."

There was some truth to that. "What is with her, anyway? I mean, why is she so nice most of the time and then she gets so evil?"

"Know what my mother says?" Mia asked. "I mean, she's really smart about things like this, and she thinks Katherine has a massive inferiority complex. Not because she was adopted, but because she thinks she's supposed to be a Remington."

"But the Remingtons don't do things like that, do they?"

"That's exactly what I said. But it's not about what the Remingtons do or don't do. It's what Katherine thinks *she* has to do in order to feel like one. It's not about what's real, Callie. It's about what's in her head."

"It's so weird."

"Yeah, but you know what?" Mia said. "It doesn't excuse the way she's treated me. I've totally had it with her. And if it's any consolation, I'm not finished with her. Not by a long shot."

Wednesday 5:38 P.M.

"VERY IMPRESSIVE, CALLIE," the man says calmly.

I feel myself go cold and tight. I recognize his face from the TV in the convenience store. It's Chief Jenkins. I glance at the door.

"No, no," he says, following my eyes. "It's over now. No more running and hiding. No more disguises." He pushes himself up from the couch and reaches into his pocket. I hear the clink of metal handcuffs. "Turn around and put your hands behind you. Don't resist. You're already in enough trouble."

I do what he says and feel the cuffs go around my wrists. Chief Jenkins recites the Miranda warning, that anything I say may be used against me. Strangely and unexpectedly, I feel relief. I don't have to hide anymore. I don't have to be constantly look-ing over my shoulder or have knots in my stomach about getting caught.

With a hand on my arm, he walks me downstairs and into the police department. The officers all stare silently. They know who I am. We go into an office with an American flag standing in the corner, bookshelves filled with ring binders, and a desk with a computer and some family pictures. In one is a young man with some tennis rackets. *His son?* I wonder.

Chief Jenkins tells me to turn around. I feel him remove the handcuffs. "Have a seat." He gestures to a chair while he sits down on the other side of the desk and pushes a phone toward me. "Call your mom."

I get Mom on the phone and have to wait while she breaks down and sobs and tells me how worried she's been. She wants to know where I've been and what's going on, but mindful of the Miranda warning, I just keep reassuring her that I'm okay and she doesn't have to worry. When she asks me when I'm coming home, all I can say is that I don't know.

The call ends with her urging me to cooperate with the police and do whatever they tell me. After all she's been through with my brother, I take the advice seriously. There's a knock on the door and a thin, balding man with a salt-and-pepper moustache sticks his head in. Before he speaks, he looks at me for longer than necessary, as if I'm something he's never seen before. Then he turns to the police chief: "PD's here."

I recognize the voice. He was the one speaking to Chief Jenkins in the lounge this morning.

The police chief turns to me. "We're going to question you, Callie. You're entitled to legal representation, and I've taken the liberty of requesting a public defender. Chief Detective Bloom will take you down to the lab."

I follow the chief detective down a hall, thinking, *Oh no, not another public defender*. We go into a police lab no larger than a closet. Inside, a policewoman asks me to open my mouth, and then rubs the inside of my cheek with several different-colored swabs. She also takes my fingerprints.

Next I'm taken to a bare room with a table, some chairs, a large mirror against one wall, and a video camera on a tripod. A woman in a black suit jacket and skirt is sitting in one of the chairs, speaking on a cell phone. She's small, maybe a few inches taller than me, and has mahogany skin and neat shoulder-length brown hair.

"That's correct, Mrs. Carson," she says into the phone while giving me the straight index finger "just a moment" sign. "Yes, of course. I'll call you as soon as I can."

She snaps the phone shut. Bloom leaves us, and the woman introduces herself as Gail and tells me she's a public defender. "So I guess you know I was just speaking to your mom."

"Uh-huh."

"She gave me permission to represent you. I've just been called on to this case, so all I know is what I've read in the news and seen on TV. What I'm going to do today is listen to each question they ask and let you know whether or not I think it's okay for you to answer. If I tell you it's okay, it's important that you answer honestly and directly. But only answer the question, Callie. Don't provide any additional information unless they specifically ask for it. And remember, they're not just asking these questions for information. Depending on how you answer them, they'll be trying to assess whether or not you're telling them the truth. So try not to do the things that make people look guilty."

"But I'm not guilty," I protest.

Gail nods perfunctorily, as if this isn't the first time some-one's said that to her. "Good. So maintain eye contact. Be aware that they'll probably repeat certain questions at different times in the interview to see if there are inconsistencies in your story."

Her attitude reminds me of that of Sebastian's public defender. They don't even *think* about trying to prove you're innocent. All they want to do is make a plea bargain and move on to the next case until they've gotten enough experience to get hired by a private law firm and start making real money.

"Ready?" Gail asks, and without waiting for my answer, she goes to the door and opens it. A moment later Chief Jenkins and Chief Detective Bloom enter. Bloom goes to the video camera, turns it on, and makes sure it's aimed at me. Then he and Chief Jenkins sit down.

"Tell us everything you remember from the night Katherine Remington-Day was murdered," Bloom says.

I turn to Gail, who nods; then I tell them what I remember. The two men take notes. When I'm finished, Chief Jenkins says, "You're certain it was Dakota Jenkins who told you to look for Katherine?"

"Yes."

"And she specifically told you to look around the dugout?"

"Yes."

Bloom asks, "Was there anyone else with her when she told you where to look?"

"I don't think so. I think she was alone. Why?"

"We need corroboration," Chief Jenkins replies. "Someone else to testify that what you're saying is true."

"But why would I lie?" I ask.

"Callie," Gail says, interrupting. "It's best to let them ask the questions. All you have to do is answer and tell the truth."

"No one's accusing you of lying, Callie," says Chief Jenkins. "This is just the way the law works. Testimony needs to be corroborated."

Bloom continues the thread: "When you went toward the dugout, did you see anyone else around there?"

I try my best to remember, then shake my head. "No."

"Did you hear anything that might have made you think someone else was there?"

"I don't think so."

Bloom and Jenkins glance at each other. The questions go on and on. What did I do when I saw Katherine's body? Why did I pick up the knife? Why did I run away? Is it true that Katherine and I were supposed to go into peer mediation? Why did I write that article for the school newspaper? Just as Gail predicted, sometimes the questions are reworded and then asked again.

"If you didn't do it, why did you run away?" Bloom asks for what must be the third time.

"I told you, I was scared. Someone took a picture of me with that knife in my hand. After what happened with my brother, I just assumed they'd think I did it."

"Okay," says Chief Jenkins. "Even if that's true, why *continue* to hide? Once you'd had a chance to calm down and think about it, why not turn yourself in then?"

I look at Gail, who nods, indicating I should answer. "Because by then I thought I knew who really did kill Katherine. And I believed the only way I could prove I didn't do it was by proving she did. But I wouldn't be able to do that if I turned myself in."

The room goes quiet. Jenkins and Bloom look at each other with grave expressions. Neither speaks. Meanwhile, Gail frowns and asks, "Who do you think killed her?"

I stare at Chief Jenkins, right into his pale hazel eyes, and say, "Your niece, Dakota."

Gail blinks with astonishment and sits back in her chair. She also looks questioningly at Chief Jenkins. "No, I'm happy to say that's not true," he says.

"How do you know?" I ask. "I bet you haven't even considered that possibility."

"Whoa!" Gail says, interrupting again, and places her hand on my arm. She gives me a concerned, quizzical look, as if it's suddenly occurred to her that I may have a few loose screws. She turns to Chief Jenkins. "Sir, I think at this point I need to familiarize myself a little more with this case. Can we continue the questioning tomorrow?"

The two men share another glance. Bloom nods. Chief Jenkins turns to Gail. "Only if you're okay with us keeping her in custody."

"You heard they caught her?"

"Uh-huh."

"I feel awful. I keep thinking that maybe if I hadn't asked her to help me . . ."

"But she didn't let on to you, right?"

"I know. That's what makes it so hard to believe."

"Just don't blame yourself, okay? You didn't know."

chapter 40

Thursday 9:35 A.M.

ONCE AGAIN IN handcuffs, I am driven to a juvenile detention facility and taken through a metal detector and several heavily reinforced doors before being placed in a cell by myself away from the rest of the inmates. Meals are brought on a tray by a silent matron, who waits and watches while I eat, and then takes the tray away.

My mother arrives with dark bags under her eyes and her hair hanging limp and unbrushed. She looks even more exhausted and worn out than usual.

In the visiting room, the matron watching us doesn't stop me from reaching over and taking my mother's hand, which feels cold and bony. She's weepy and bewildered and doesn't understand why the police won't let me go. All I can do is reassure her. "It's going to be okay, Mom. I promise. Everything's going to work out. If they really thought I did it, they would have arrested me, right? They're just holding on to me to make sure I tell them everything I know."

After a while, Mom says that she has to go home and take care of Dad, and that she'll come back tomorrow if I'm still here. I ask her to bring some clean clothes. In the afternoon I am driven back to the police station and taken to the interrogation room, where I am joined by Gail and the two men. Once again they ask me questions about Katherine, about what I did the night she was killed, and about what had happened between us in the weeks leading up to that night.

The questioning lasts several hours, and then the camera is turned off. The men leave and Gail and I are alone.

"How much longer are they going to keep asking the same questions?" I ask.

"Until they decide whether you're telling the truth," Gail explains. "Since yesterday, I've been able to learn a little more about the case, and I have to tell you honestly, Callie, it's a very difficult situation. They have a lot of evidence against you."

I feel my spirits sink. It sounds like she's paving the way to a plea bargain. Only there's something I still don't understand. "Then why do they keep questioning me? Why don't they just . . . ?"

"Arrest you and charge you with the murder?" It sounds horrible when she says it out loud. "I'm not one hundred percent sure, Callie. Part of the reason, I suspect, is that there were no witnesses. So most of the evidence the police have is circumstantial. The other part may be that you've stuck to your story consistently, and no matter how many times they ask, you give them the same answers. And, in a trial, that could be enough to raise reasonable doubt."

"Then why don't they let me go?"

"I assume it's because they're still trying to build a case," Gail says. "Under the law they can hold you for up to seventy-two hours. And I think they're determined to do that, because you've demonstrated such a talent for avoiding capture. They're afraid if they let you go, they may never see you again."

There's an irony, I can't help thinking.

Gail clears her throat in an awkward way, and I sense there's something else on her mind. "Listen, Callie, there's something . . . I need to toss out to you just because . . . well, because I want to be completely honest with you. Based on the evidence they've shown me, I think we should at least consider the possibility that they may still charge and arrest you in Katherine's murder. It would be foolish for us not to consider the possibility and start preparing for it."

Why am I not surprised to hear her say this? "Prepare for it how?" I ask, because I know that's what she expects.

"By considering the option of claiming it was self-defense."

Huh? It takes a moment for me to grasp what she's saying. Claiming self-defense means admitting I killed Katherine. It's saying that she attacked me and I fought back, and in the process she died. "So, it's like a plea bargain, right?"

"Well . . ." She hesitates. "Not exactly. You're not pleading guilty to anything."

"Except *killing* her," I point out.

"In self-defense."

"But that's not what happened," I answer.

It's difficult to read Gail's expression. I wonder if lawyers are taught to hide what they're thinking. She leans forward, her gold hoop earrings swinging gently. "Callie, as a public defender it's my job to represent you in the best way I know possible. Given the amount of evidence they have—the photo, the fingerprints on the knife—it may be difficult for a jury to believe you had nothing to do with the murder. However, I believe, based on your history with Katherine, specifically what happened in school, that we can make an argument that she attacked you and you defended yourself."

I'm stunned. She's saying I can go free . . . by *admitting* I killed Katherine. By doing the *exact opposite* of what I know I should do. It's crazy. "What about Dakota? What about Griffen Clemment and the threatening texts?"

"His parents have hired a defense attorney. Griffen isn't talking."

"Doesn't it mean he's hiding something?" I ask.

"Not necessarily. He could be completely innocent, and his parents are just being careful. From what I hear, they can afford it. But it doesn't matter. The police have got the record of the text messages he received. But we haven't been able to link the phone they were sent from to Dakota Jenkins."

"But who else would have sent them? They *have* to have come from her."

Gail shrugs. "The law doesn't work that way. We need real evidence linking Dakota to the phone that sent those texts and we don't have it."

"Then what about the knife that should be missing from the set at the Jenkinses' home?"

Gail looks down at the table and then back at me. "I spoke to Congresswoman Jenkins. She checked the set of knives you talked about. They're all there. She's not missing any."

"That can't be! She's lying! She knows what Dakota did and she's trying to protect her. All they had to do was go out and buy a replacement knife. I'm telling you she—"

Gail raises her hand, gesturing for me to stop. "Callie, what made you think the knife came from Dakota's house?"

"It was a special brand," I explain. "I . . . The only time I've ever seen it was in Dakota's kitchen. I can't remember the name now, but it had two little stick-figure men against a red square background."

Gail purses her lips sympathetically. "The brand is called Henckels, and to be honest, Callie, it's not that special. Lots of people have them."

chapter 41

Friday 9:47 A.M.

THERE'S A CHANCE I can go free.

All I have to do is pretend I killed Katherine.

I spent another night in juvie, despondent and miserable. Gail says that if I don't agree to the self-defense idea, it's possible that I could spend the next ten or fifteen years in prison. But how do you *pretend* you killed someone?

I'm taken to the visitors' room again. Only this time my mother is waiting there with Gail. Mom's hair is brushed and she's even wearing a little makeup. She's got a smile on her face, but I know her well enough to suspect it's forced.

"What's going on?" I ask suspiciously as soon as I sit down. Mom and Gail share a pensive glance. Now I know for certain they're up to something.

"Honey, Gail told me about her idea," Mom says.

A sense of betrayal hurtles through me. It may not be rational, but I'm furious at Gail, who has obviously brought my mother here to try to persuade me to agree to claim self-defense.

"But I didn't kill her!" I cry. "You can't—"

Gail raises her hand to quiet me. "Callie, you have to put it in perspective."

"You want me to put it in perspective?" I shoot back angrily, and turn to Mom. "She's using you. She wants me to pretend I killed Katherine because it's way too much work to try to prove I'm innocent. Just like when that jerk who defended Sebastian wanted him to plead to attempted manslaughter. Is that what *you* want, Mom? Do you want the world to think that your son attempted murder and your daughter killed someone in self-defense?"

"Yes," Mom replies calmly.

After the article came out in the school newspaper, I found myself in the same position as Dakota, spending lunchtime in the library rather than face Katherine. The first day I went to the library, Dakota was sitting at the computer table. I sat on a couch near the fiction section and we didn't speak.

But the next day I decided I wanted to talk and started toward her. As soon as Dakota realized what I was doing, she got up and walked toward the back of the library, where the tall stacks of books were.

It didn't take a nuclear physicist to figure out that she didn't want to be seen talking to me.

She went down one aisle of bookshelves and I went down the next. We stood facing each other with the shelves between us and pretended to be looking at books.

"Nice article," Dakota whispered sarcastically, as if she

knew that was why I was in the library and not the cafeteria.

"Thanks," I answered, emphasizing it with a groan.

"I can't believe the way you singled out Katherine."

"First of all, I didn't write it alone," I said, and explained that I'd written it with Mia and that it was supposed to have both our names on it. "She asked me to help her. I was just trying to be supportive. And second, it wasn't meant to be about Katherine. We were writing about a trend."

Through the shelves, Dakota gave me a "get real" look. "The thing about how it used to be that kids had to be good at something, but now all you need is to be born rich? Jodie acts and does ads. Zelda's the captain of the girls' volleyball team. Everyone knows I'm going to run for president of the student council. The only one who did nothing except be born rich, who never runs for an office where she has to be elected, and who isn't involved with sports is Katherine."

"It still wasn't supposed to single her out," I insisted.

"Maybe not, but that's *exactly* what it did," Dakota said, then leaned closer and dropped her voice even more. "Just between you and me? I'm glad *you* did it."

The way she said "you" made me think she meant that it was something she'd wanted to do, too. "Why?"

"Because now the rumors she's spreading are about you, not me."

"What rumors?"

Dakota smiled, but it wasn't a friendly smile. "About the night before school started? About you and two guys at once."

"That's—" I started to react, but the outrage passed quickly.

"That's lame. Everyone'll know she's just trying to get back at me."

"Maybe." Dakota shrugged.

Since we were speaking confidentially, I decided to bring up the reason I'd wanted to talk to her. "What happened between you two?"

"Nothing."

"You can't stand her being more popular than you?" I asked, pressing her.

Dakota lifted her eyes to the ceiling. "Oh, please, that's *so* seventh grade."

"Then what?" I asked. "Why can't you be honest with me?"

After a moment of silence, she said, "Look, Callie, I'm never going to confide in you. You and I are never going to be friends, okay? It's just not happening."

And then she walked away.

chapter 42

IN THE VISITORS' room, Mom's answer nearly knocks me off my chair. I stare at her in utter disbelief.

"If it means," Mom continues, "that I won't have to visit two children in jail."

That's how she sees it, plain and simple. I slump down, feeling defeated. Talk about getting the wind knocked out of you. This can't be real. It's a nightmare, a horror movie.

Gail leans closer. "Callie, think for a moment. What's our goal here?"

"*My* goal is to prove I didn't kill Katherine," I snap. "*Your* goal is probably to plea bargain this thing in time for lunch."

"Callie!" Mom gasps, horrified, and then turns to Gail. "I'm so sorry. She doesn't mean that."

I roll my eyes, letting Gail know I most assuredly do mean it.

"That's not my goal," Gail replies calmly. "My goal is to keep you from going to jail." She pauses and waits, as if the words need time to sink into my incredibly thick skull. "Claiming self-defense is considerably better than a plea bargain, because it means no jail time. So I understand that it sounds crazy and backwards and upside down, Callie, but it's your best shot."

"But I didn't kill her!" I ball my hands into fists as tears of frustration well up in my eyes. I can't stand this! It's *so* unfair!

Mom leans forward and places her hand over mine. "Honey, please. Gail's told me about the article you wrote and how angry Katherine was. It makes sense that she could have been angry enough to attack you."

I stare at her in complete shock. My own mother is telling me to lie. To pretend I killed someone when I didn't. It's incomprehensible. Mom turns to Gail. "Let me speak to her alone, okay?"

Gail gets up and walks to the far side of the visitors' room. Still holding my hand, Mom leans close. I feel an intensity and urgency from her that I'm not used to. "Listen to me, Callie," she says in a low, firm voice. "You're young, and young people tend to see everything in black and white, right and wrong. But as you get older, you'll see that the lines get blurred, and a lot of what you thought was either black or white is simply gray. You're a smart girl. You know things change. People change. Their outlooks change. Even if you can't understand what I'm saying now, I promise that someday you will. You have to believe me on this. A lot of life is about compromising. Usually someone your age doesn't have to compromise on anything nearly this serious. But you've already faced a lot of things someone your age shouldn't have to face. So maybe you can look at this as just one more of those things."

Her grip on my hand is tight. I know she's seen a lot more of life than I have and knows a lot more than I do. And she loves me and would never suggest I do anything that would be bad for me. So I tell her I'll think about it.

And I mean it.

Before she and Gail go, Mom gives me a paper bag with clean clothes and I ask her to call Slade and tell him where I am. Tell him that if he can come, I'd really like to see him.

A few days after the article was in the school newspaper, Dr. Ploumis, the school psychologist, called me to her office. I walked in and there was David Sloan. I stopped, confused.

"Have a seat, Callie," Dr. Ploumis said.

I sat down, looking back and forth from the school psychologist to David.

"Callie, as you know, there's been a lot of talk about the article you wrote," Dr. Ploumis began. "And you know that Katherine is extremely upset."

"And what about the rumors about me she's been spreading?" I asked defensively, since it sounded to me like I was the one who was going to be blamed.

"Yes, I've heard about that, too," said Dr. Ploumis. "And that's why I asked David to join us. You're aware that he's the peer mediation leader for your class."

I wasn't. Of course, I'd heard of peer mediation, but it was something I'd never taken seriously. To me it sounded like just one more extracurricular activity that would look good on a college application.

"I think that you and Katherine should settle your differences through peer mediation," Dr. Ploumis said.

"I don't think that's necessary," I said. "I mean, nobody really believes those rumors. Everyone knows why Katherine's spreading them."

Dr. Ploumis gave me a funny look. "That's not really the point, Callie. The point is that you and Katherine have very public issues that have not been resolved. The whole school is aware of them, and that makes it a good example of the kind of thing peer mediation was created to resolve."

"So that's what this is about?" I asked. "Using us as an example of how peer mediation can work?"

"No, and yes," the school psychologist replied. "The primary reason is to settle this dispute. But yes, secondarily, it would be a useful example. It's not like everyone isn't already aware of what's going on. After all, it was your decision to write that article and publish it in the *Bugle*."

For a second I considered telling her that it wasn't my idea. It was Mia's. But what good would that do? It wouldn't take the blame off me, and it would probably cost me another friend. So instead, I said, "And of course, there's just no way in the world that you'll ever believe that article had nothing to do with Katherine."

Dr. Ploumis and David exchanged glances, as if they'd known that was what I'd say. I really didn't like the way they seemed to be ganging up on me.

"It almost doesn't matter now what your intention was," Dr. Ploumis said. "The reality is that no matter what you intended, everyone, including Katherine, believes you wrote the article about her. And I feel that it's important that you two sit down and discuss it face-to-face."

David leaned forward. "Katherine's already said she's willing to meet."

"Oh, great," I said, annoyed that they'd already conspired on this. "So now I have no choice. If I say no, it just makes me look even worse."

"Callie, no one is trying to make you look bad," Dr. Ploumis said. "We're just trying to resolve a situation that needs resolution."

I believed her, but I wondered if David had told her everything she needed to know. "Okay, I'll agree to meet, but are you sure David should be involved?"

Both of them frowned.

"Why not?" asked Dr. Ploumis.

I turned to David. "Did you tell her about you and Katherine?"

David's eyebrows dipped deeper. "What about us?"

"I heard you had a thing with her last year," I said. "She asked you to the Sadie Hawkins dance and the next night you two went into a bedroom at a party and you did something she didn't like and then at school she told Mia to go over and slap you."

David's mouth fell open.

Dr. Ploumis gave him a quizzical look. "Is that true?"

"No way! I don't know what you're talking about," he said. "Katherine asked me to the Sadie Hawkins dance and then spent the whole night with her friends. And I never went into any bedrooms with her. And I have no idea why she sent Mia to slap me, other than to prove that she could."

It sounded like he was telling the truth. And the more I thought about it, the less I felt that he had reason to lie. So I agreed to meet for peer mediation during lunch on the following Monday. But I couldn't help wondering where that story about David and Katherine in the bedroom had come from.

Not that it mattered. By Monday, Katherine was dead.

Friday 11:51 A.M.

I'M ALLOWED TO take a shower and change into the clean clothes Mom brought. Then I'm sent back to my cell to wait and think about what Mom and Gail want me to do. Even though I know I should consider what Mom said, it's practically impossible. How can I agree to say it was self-defense?

I hardly touch lunch. Who could possibly eat at a time like this? Later a matron comes to my cell. I assume she's going to transport me back to the town center for another round of questions, but instead, she says, "You have a visitor."

My heart leaps, and my spirits skyrocket. It's Slade! He must have just heard from Mom and come right over! I've missed him so much. The memories of that kiss in the lounge and of his saying he'd always love me are the only bright spots in my life.

I practically skip out of the cell and down the hall.

Will I be allowed to kiss him?

Hug him?

But the person waiting for me at the round table in the visitors' room is Chief Jenkins. "Have a seat, Callie."

I slump into a chair, not bothering to hide my disappointment.

"You were expecting someone else?"

I shrug, struggling to hold back the tears that unexpectedly threaten to burst forth.

"Slade Lamont?"

I look up, surprised, and feel the moisture gathering in my eyes. My emotions are so raw and torn that I can't muster the strength to hide them anymore. Tears roll down my cheeks. Chief Jenkins nods, as if I've just answered his question. "So, I guess you're wondering why I'm here."

I don't bother to answer or even nod. Obviously he wouldn't be here if he wasn't going to tell me. He takes off his hat and places it on the table. The hat leaves a reddish ridge across his forehead. "I came here to tell you a story about your father, Callie. Something I suspect you don't know."

I have absolutely no idea what he's going to say.

"A long time ago he and I were friends," Chief Jenkins says. "Pretty close, actually. You didn't know that, did you?"

I shake my head. Dad never said a word about it. I wonder if it's true or just some new trick they're playing to get me to admit to other things that aren't true.

"I'm not surprised," Chief Jenkins goes on. "We had a pretty bad falling-out. And after that, we never really spoke to each other again."

He pauses as if waiting for me to ask what happened. But

I don't. He's come here to tell me a story. Be my guest. "We were both on the Soundview High tennis team."

I stare at him uncertainly. *Tennis?* I remember Mom saying something about Dad's being on the team. I meant to ask him why he quit, but I never did.

"We were tremendous rivals in high school," the police chief continues. "At least, he thought we were. I played first singles on the team, and all he wanted to do was beat me and play first singles himself."

I'm still not sure whether to believe any of this. But if I do, then obviously I have to believe that my father couldn't beat Chief Jenkins. Otherwise, what would be the point of his telling me this?

The police chief goes on: "For some reason I was born with athletic talent coming out of my ears. Great reflexes. Amazing hand-eye coordination. The funny thing was, I couldn't have cared less. I played on my high-school teams—tennis, baseball, basketball—but I knew I wouldn't play in college. I had other things in mind. Your father couldn't have been more different. What he lacked in raw talent he tried to make up for with determination, practice, training, and studying. He would practice and practice, study strategy, read all the books, and then challenge me. But I would always beat him. Well, that's not really true. Most of the time he would beat himself. Psych himself out. Truth is, he was what we used to call a head case."

Well, at least that part rings true. So now I'm becoming curious. "What happened?"

Chief Jenkins runs his thick fingers back over his thin hair as if checking to make sure those few black strands are still there. "I called a let."

"Sorry?" I'm not sure I know what he means.

"When you serve and the ball nicks the net but still goes in the service box, it's called a let. You get to do the serve over. Anyway, your dad challenged me to a match. And as usual he acted as if it wasn't just some dumb tennis game but was practically a matter of life and death. As if his entire future depended on it. So we got into a fight over a ball I thought was a let. And your dad just . . . went . . . nuts."

I nod. It's so easy to imagine Dad doing that.

"Finally, he called me a cheater and walked off the court, quit the team, and never talked to me again. And, as far as I know, he never played tennis again, either."

I'm struck by how sincerely sad and filled with regret Chief Jenkins appears to be. As if, while he didn't care that much about tennis, he really cared about my dad. But I still don't understand why he's telling me this.

He goes on: "After high school, I went into the army for two years and then to the police academy. Even though he wouldn't talk to me, I kept tabs on your dad, so I know he went to FCC. And then, later, when we'd both gotten married and I'd moved back here, I'd hear stories about him and the troubles he had with your brother. Especially since Sebastian had had a few run-ins with us, as well. I'd see your dad from time to time, but he'd never do more than nod. He was a very angry guy. Always at war with someone or something."

Chief Jenkins levels his eyes on me and I recognize it as a

caring gaze. His eyes are sad, as if he's seen too many things he wishes he hadn't seen. He places his left hand on the table. He's wearing a wedding ring. "So, you're surely wondering why I'm telling you all this," he finally says. "I guess . . . it goes back to when your dad and I were friends. Just that he'd always wanted so badly the things I'd been given without even asking. I guess . . . I always felt bad for him. It seemed like he caught a lot of unlucky breaks."

He pauses again. From some other part of the facility come distant shouts followed by laughter. Not what you'd expect in a detention center. Meanwhile, I'm still waiting, wondering why he's told me all this and where the story's going. But I sense I won't have to wonder for much longer. He places his right arm on the table, leans toward me, and lowers his voice. "I hear you're refusing to go along with the self-defense argument."

He gazes steadily at me, waiting for my reply. I fold my hands in my lap and look straight into his eyes, as if to say if that's why he's here, he's wasting his time, but what comes out of my mouth is "Why would I agree to claim self-defense when I'm innocent?"

Chief Jenkins looks down at his hat, lying on the table, and turns it slightly with his finger. "Callie, suppose I told you . . . we think the knife . . . came from Katherine's house?" His eyes rise again to meet mine.

What? I rock back in the chair as if he's pushed me. It makes no sense. Why would Katherine bring the knife to the kegger? "How could that be?"

"To be honest, we're not sure. But let's forget that for a moment. Would just knowing the knife came from her house

228

make you more comfortable about pleading self-defense?"

I feel like he's practically rolling out a red carpet for me. If Katherine brought the knife, it might imply that she wanted to kill me. So then claiming self-defense would make perfect sense. I'd go free. No one could blame me for defending myself. I'd be with Slade again.

Only it would still mean admitting I killed Katherine.

"I have to tell you, Callie, I don't understand why you won't agree to it," Chief Jenkins says. "There were no witnesses. If you say it was self-defense, there's no one who can really argue. It adds the crucial element of doubt. It's almost impossible to imagine a jury convicting you in that situation. On the other hand, if you insist on your innocence, you know you're making it much more difficult for the jury. They know someone killed Katherine Remington-Day, and a lot of the evidence points to you. In that situation, I can't predict what they'll decide, and neither can anyone else. But the possibility of being convicted of second-degree murder, and serving a long prison term, is much *much* greater."

Yes, I've heard this before. So why is he telling me again? Is it a trick? Is he trying to get me to plead self-defense because it will take away the possibility that Dakota will be accused? That could be it, right? But something tells me it isn't. I may be only seventeen and not old enough to be a great judge of character, but I feel that I am looking into the eyes of a man who is telling the truth.

"Maybe you're not responding because your lawyer told you not to talk to anyone and the Miranda warning states that anything you do say may be used against you," Chief Jenkins continues. "But I want you to understand something, Callie. My duty as an officer of the law is to seek justice. I've taken an oath to fulfill that duty to the best of my abilities. But I also have a commitment to the people of this community to do what I believe is best for all involved. It's not to decide whether you are innocent or guilty. That's up to a judge and jury. But I've known your family for a long time, and personally, I think you've faced more than enough hardships. Maybe you could think of it this way— I've come here today not as the chief of police but as a friend who doesn't understand why you'd want to risk another tragedy when there's such an obvious way around it."

I know I'm not supposed to say anything, but I can't help it. I stare him right in those watery hazel eyes and ask, "Have you ever been accused of something you didn't do?"

He blinks as if this isn't what he expected me to say. "Yes."

"Then you know how it feels."

He gazes at me for a long time with an expression that at first seems astonished and then turns thoughtful. "You had nothing to do with Katherine Remington-Day's murder?"

"Nothing whatsoever."

"There was no plan? You weren't in it with someone else? You never discussed it with anyone?"

"Discussed what? I have no idea what you're even talking about. It's like there's something else going on here that no one will tell me about. What is it?"

"Did Mia Flom ever tell you she was going to get Katherine?"

Was *that* why she came out of the police station with her father and that woman lawyer?

"She might have said something like that," I answer. "But . . . it never sounded like—"

"Did she ever mention physical threats?"

"I . . . I don't remember."

The police chief drums his fingers against the table. "Did you go to Jerry Fairman's house a few nights ago?"

I'm so eager to prove my innocence that I almost say I did, but then I catch myself. I don't know what Jerry has to do with any of this, but he did me a big favor. He did my brother a much, much bigger favor. Whatever he had to do with the trap at the train station, I have to believe he was forced into it. I don't want to get him into trouble. I stare down at the table mutely.

Chief Jenkins studies me a moment longer and then nods as if he's made up his mind about something. "I've been in this profession a long time, Callie. I like to think that I've gotten pretty good at separating the liars from those who are telling the truth." Then he picks up his hat, places his hands on the table, and heaves himself up. "That's all I have to say."

chapter 44

Friday 10:34 P.M.

ANOTHER NIGHT IN juvie to think about what people said and what they might have meant. A plan? In it with someone else? What was Chief Jenkins talking about? What could Jerry have to do with this? And how could the knife have come from Katherine's house?

For the hundredth time I go over it in my head, replaying everything that's happened. No, that's not quite true. There's one memory I always avoid unless someone, like Gail or Chief Jenkins, makes me think about it—that horrible scene of finding Katherine dead.

But tonight I force myself to go back over it. Her body on the ground. The others coming. Their dark silhouettes. Dakota saying, "You killed her!" The flash of the camera . . . the blur of faces.

But wait. The faces aren't really a blur. They're kids I know. Kids from school . . .

. . . except the tall one with blond hair—

And suddenly I know why Griffen Clemment looked familiar. He was there that night, in that crowd.

Griffen, who said he hadn't spoken to Katherine or Dakota since the previous spring.

Did he play a role in Katherine's death?

I go over it in my head again and again, but I can't make sense of it.

And I fall asleep knowing that there's still so much I don't know.

But something is different when I wake in the morning. I don't know why or how, but during the night, I've made peace with the idea of pleading self-defense. Maybe because I've realized how much I don't know. But what I do know is that Mom and Chief Jenkins want me to do it.

And what if Slade also wanted me to do it? Would I? For him?

Yes, I think maybe in that case I would.

Later a matron appears outside my cell. I'm once again filled with hope that Slade has come to see me. But she says, "Take everything you want, because you're not coming back."

What? I stare at her, confused.

"You're out," she says. "Free to go."

I don't understand, but I'm not about to argue. The matron escorts me down the hall and through the reinforced doors. Gail is sitting in the waiting room, wearing a gray raincoat. She rises and smiles and, seeing the confusion on my face, explains: "The seventy-two hours is up. They haven't decided to press charges, so you can go."

"Ser . . . iously?" I'm so filled with surprise and disbelief that I can hardly get the word out of my mouth.

"Well, sort of," Gail says as we start to walk toward the exit. "As a condition of your release, I had to make two promises. But I don't think you'll be bothered by either of them."

It's raining. As we walk to the parking lot, she opens an umbrella. "You have to wear an ankle monitor. So they know where you are in case they want to talk to you again."

"Or arrest me?"

"I suppose it can't be ruled out."

"What's the other promise?"

"Under no circumstances are you to leave the county."

"What difference does it make if I'm wearing an ankle monitor? Won't they know where I am anyway?"

Gail bugs her eyes at me. "Why are you giving me grief? You're out, okay? Free! All you have to do is wear the stupid thing and not leave the county. When's the last time you left the county, anyway?"

She's right. For the first time in what feels like forever, I have a smile on my face.

We stop at the police station and they place the monitor just above my right ankle. It's a black box, slightly smaller than a pack of cigarettes, on a black strap. The officer who puts it on warns me that even though I could cut it off with scissors, as soon as I did, I'd break the circuit and send an alarm to the tracking unit.

Then Gail drops me off at my house. Stepping through the front door feels strange, as if I've been gone for months, not days. It's dim and cool inside. Mom's become fanatical about keeping the lights off and the heat down while she tries to get by on Dad's disability payments.

"Mom?" I call from the front hall.

"Callie?" Coming from the kitchen, her voice is filled with surprise. A moment later she appears in the hallway in her old red plaid robe and envelops me in her arms. "Thank God!"

She's so happy that I'm home that she hardly seems to hear when I explain what's happened and why they let me go. All she cares about is that I'm free. As soon as I can get away from her, I go to a phone and call Slade, but I get his voice mail. He's probably at the town center, finishing the job. I'd text him from Mom's phone, but she doesn't have texting set up. I could wait for him to call me back, but I'm too excited, too brimming with yearning to see him. I beg Mom to let me borrow the car. Just to go into town. Please? She finally says yes and I drive to the town center.

Slade's pickup isn't in the parking lot, but maybe he parked somewhere else or rode with his dad that morning. I go through the back door of the center and follow the sounds of hammers and saws up to the second floor. In the hallway a painter lugging a large white bucket stops and stares at me like he's seeing a ghost.

"Do you know where the Lamonts are?" I ask.

He points down the hall and I go in that direction, looking through doorways into empty rooms until I come to one and see Mr. Lamont's back. With quick, deft movements, he's using a trowel of mud to fill the seams and screw holes along a new wall. I watch for a moment, then say, "Hi."

Mr. Lamont stops and turns. A day or two's worth of gray stubble coats his jaw, and his broad stomach hangs over his belt. This is a man who always has a smile on his face for me. But there's no smile today. "Hello, Callie."

"Is Slade here?"

He doesn't answer. His eyes slide away and his face grows sadder. Something's wrong and I feel myself fill with dread even before he answers: "He's gone."

"Gone?" I repeat. I can tell by the way he says it that he doesn't mean gone to the store. He means gone. My mind screens the possibilities. "Not deployed? He said he'd been—"

Mr. Lamont shakes his head. "Just gone. Cleaned out his bank account and left a note saying good-bye and not to bother looking for him."

This makes no sense. *Where* would he go? I feel my heart begin to disintegrate. "That's all it said?" I ask, thinking, *Nothing about me?*

"It said to tell you he was sorry."

"About what?"

"I don't know, Callie. I wish I did, but I don't."

I'm back in the car and driving down the thruway. Mom's going to have a fit when I don't bring the car back. The police are going to go ballistic when they figure out I've left the county, but I don't care. I have to find him.

chapter 45

Saturday 8:37 P.M.

IT'S DARK AND the rain is coming down hard. My hair is soaked. As I walk across a parking lot, water drips down my neck and sends chills as it runs down my back. My feet are soaked and cold from stepping into puddles. The smell of fish and ocean is in my nose as I pull open a door. This is the twelfth bar I've gone into. The odor of stale beer is in the air. Yellowish light inside illuminates half a dozen grizzled men hunched over drinks. TVs on the walls at either end show a baseball game.

I peer through the gloomy shadows at the booths along the walls, expecting the same result as I got at the past eleven places. But there's one person sitting in a booth by himself, wearing a baseball cap. It's dark in here and I can't be sure, but it could be him.

A moment later I'm standing beside the booth. On the table are an empty shot glass, a half-finished beer, and a laptop computer with a ragged piece of tape where my photo used to be. Feeling a presence nearby, he glances up casually, then does a major-league double take. He looks utterly astonished as I slide into the booth, across from him, then reach over the table and take his hand in mine.

"You . . . you remembered," he says.

I nod. "That night you called, so excited."

He lifts the baseball cap off his head, then replaces it, as if he needed to let the heat out. "They let you go?"

"Uh-huh. Aren't you happy to see me?"

He looks surprised, than squeezes my hand. "Oh, yeah! I mean, yes, of course I'm happy about that, Cal. It's just . . ."

"Just what?"

Instead of answering, he changes the subject. "I heard they were trying to get you to claim it was self-defense."

"I would have . . . for you. But they didn't press charges."

Slade's eyes go blank. I thought he'd be happy to hear that, happy to see me, but now his forehead bunches. "You . . . *didn't* agree to say it was self-defense?"

"I just told you I didn't have to. Aren't you happy? Slade, I don't understand what's going on. Why did you leave? I thought you said you were going to stay."

He gazes at me with eyes that turn sad, then places his other hand over mine. Now both of mine are in both of his and he leans over the table and presses his forehead against my knuckles. It seems as if he's just realized something. What is it he's not telling me? I wonder. What is it that I still don't know? But now that I'm with him, I don't have to press. He'll tell me when he's ready. "So that's the deal. It's okay. I'm glad you came. Really, you don't know how happy I am to see you."

"You don't *sound* happy," I tell him.

He leans back in the booth, takes a deep breath, and lets it out, then finishes the beer in one gulp. "Come on, Shrimp, let's get out of here."

When word of a kegger began to circulate, Mia called up and asked me to go with her. I said I didn't think I'd feel like it.

"You can't hide forever," she said.

"I'm not," I said, although that wasn't true. I'd been going to the library every day at lunch.

"So why haven't I seen you in the cafeteria?" she said. "Listen, Callie, I want you to come to the kegger. I want people to see us together so they know I'm on your side."

Slade and I spend the night in his motel room. I'm so happy to feel his arms around me, to feel his lips on my neck and face and mouth, to hear him tell me he loves me, to be able to tell him I love him and know he believes me, and finally, to fall asleep with my head on his shoulder.

BANGING ON THE door. "It's the police! Open up!"

My eyes burst open. Beside me, Slade's are already wide. Thin shafts of sunlight seep in around the curtains.

"Come on, open the door." I recognize the voice. It's Chief Jenkins.

"Don't try to go out the bathroom window. We've got a man back there."

Slade's staring at me with a startled look. I slide my arms around his warm body and give him a hug, but he's as frozen as a statue. "It's okay," I whisper to reassure him. "I knew this was going to happen. They tracked the ankle monitor, but at least I got to see you."

"Ankle monitor?"

"Yeah, they made me wear it, but I cut it off in the bathroom last night. I didn't want to freak you out."

"Slade, Callie, we know you're in there. Open up!"

Slade goes limp. "Oh, Shrimp." He sounds so sad.

This isn't the way I want it to be. I want him to squeeze me in his arms and tell me that he'll love me forever. "It's okay." I kiss him on the lips. "Really, Slade, you can relax. Everything's going to work out."

"Slade! Callie!"

But it doesn't seem as if Slade can respond. It's like he's in shock. Like he can't believe this is really happening.

Louder, more insistent banging on the door. "Open up!"

"I'm coming," I call, then give Slade one last kiss and whisper, "I love you. And no matter what happens, I'll always love you." As I get out of bed, I turn to the door and say, "Just give me one second."

"Come on!" Chief Jenkins demands impatiently.

I pull on my clothes, then turn to Slade. He's sitting up now, on the edge of the bed, his head hanging as he stares at the floor. "Listen," I whisper, "it's going to be okay. I swear."

The banging on the door grows louder. "Come out now or we break it down!"

"Okay, I'm coming." I go to the door and open it. The sun is just rising and some clouds overhead are pink. Chilly ocean air flows in and I have to shield my eyes from the brightness. Chief Jenkins and a police officer in uniform are standing there. The police chief stares at me, then past me at Slade, who's still on the edge of the bed.

"I'm sorry," I tell him. "I know I wasn't supposed to leave the county, but I had to. You can take me back now. It's okay." I even turn around with my hands behind me so that he can put on the cuffs.

But that's not what happens. I feel him step past me, followed by the uniformed officer, as they go to the bed where Slade sits.

"Put on some clothes," Chief Jenkins orders.

Slade reaches to the floor and starts to pull on his pants.

The police chief recites, "Slade Lamont, you are being arrested for the murder of Katherine Remington-Day. You have the right to remain silent. Anything you say can and will be used against you in a court of law. You have the right to an attorney. If you cannot afford an attorney, one will be appointed to you. Do you understand these rights as they have been read to you?"

Mia picked me up and we went to the kegger, parking in the dark lot beside the baseball field. "I'm glad you're doing this," she said. "I mean, I'm glad *we're* doing this. You won't be sorry you came. We'll have fun."

The truth was I was starting to believe her and was looking forward to the party. It had to be better than spending another night at home. We walked into the woods, following voices and glimmers of red cigarette embers. There were probably forty or fifty people there. It was dark and they were mostly just silhouettes, but almost instantly I saw a group of girls. Brianna and Zelda, being tall, stood out. And their presence meant the others no doubt included Katherine and Jodie.

I stopped, turned to Mia, and whispered, "I thought you said she wasn't going to be here."

"I—I didn't think she would," Mia stammered.

I rolled my eyes. "Has anyone ever told you that you are the most unconvincing liar ever?"

She grinned sheepishly. "Okay, I didn't want you to stay away because of her. I want you to stand up to her with me."

At that point it no longer mattered. Thanks to peer mediation, I'd be not only standing up to Katherine, but face-to-face with her the following Monday.

Not that we really stood up to her at the kegger anyway. We just didn't cross paths. After a while, Mia went off, but by then I was hanging out with other kids. She was right. I did have fun . . . until later, when Dakota came up and said Katherine was missing.

Standing near the motel-room door, I feel my entire body go rigid. The air leaves my lungs and I can't seem to find a new breath. I feel a chill all over, then pins and needles, then cold sweat. What are they talking about? What's going on? I don't understand. They've made a mistake. Slade isn't the one they want. It's me they want.

"Yes," Slade answers to the police chief's question about his rights, but he's not looking at Chief Jenkins. He's looking at me, his skin pale, his hands shaking as he buckles his pants.

He pulls on a shirt, but before he can even begin buttoning it, the uniformed officer spins him around and applies handcuffs to his wrists, then takes him by the arm and starts to lead him toward the door. But I can't let him go. It makes no sense. It's all wrong! "Wait!" I cry, blocking their path and sliding my arms around Slade's waist and pressing my cheek against his bare chest. "You're wrong! He had nothing to do with it!"

"Let go of him, Callie," Chief Jenkins says calmly.

"*No!*" The cry that leaves my throat comes from the deepest depths of my soul. They can't arrest Slade! It's a mistake! I won't let them! I look up at him, imploring him. "Please! They're wrong! Slade, tell them!"

But with his hands cuffed behind him and my arms around him, Slade doesn't move or speak. For a moment, everything is still. Then Chief Jenkins gently says, "Let go, Callie."

I'm still looking up at Slade. Tears have begun to roll down his cheeks.

And that's when I know it's true.

chapter 47

THERE WAS A boy who lived with his mother and father and older brother and sister. They were a happy family until one day when his mother was too tired to get out of bed. And then everything began to change. No one spoke about it in front of the boy, but the mood in the house became tense and sad, and his father's and older brother's and sister's faces were always grim. His mother went to the hospital and his sister cried when she made the boy his breakfast and packed him off to school the way his mother used to do.

And the boy felt sad.

His mother came home a few weeks later and soon lost all her hair and took to wearing scarves and hats. She started making his breakfasts again, but often by dinnertime, she was too exhausted to cook. At first there were still moments when she was happy and full of energy, but gradually they were outweighed by days when she was exhausted and the house was gloomy and quiet.

It went on that way for a while, and then one day his mother went back to the hospital. A few days later the boy's father took him to the hospital and the boy saw sad faces on the nurses and doctors when he went down the hall, holding his father's hand. The boy and his father went into a room and there was his mother in bed, only she looked more like a grandmother and was now wrinkled and pale and thin. She held his hand and cried and the boy knew something very bad was happening.

Then the boy's father walked with him back to the car and it was the first time the boy had ever seen his father cry. And the boy felt very, very sad.

At the funeral, with many crying people, the boy watched his mother's casket go into the ground, but it was hard to believe that she was really inside it.

For a while the boy lived in his house without a mother, and his father and sister and brother tried to do the things his mother had done, but of course, they could not do any of them as well. And then a new woman started to come around, and after a while, the boy was introduced to her children, and then one day there was a big party and the woman and her children moved in with them.

At first things seemed better again. His father was happier. The new woman wasn't the same as the boy's mother, but by then the boy understood that his mother wasn't coming back. So he tried to pretend that the woman would be his new mother and he tried to get along with his new brothers and sisters. Then the new woman had a baby and suddenly the boy had a half sister named Alyssa.

A few years passed and then his father wasn't happy anymore and there was yelling and fighting—things the boy had never heard at home before.

And then the new woman and her children left, and while things at home once again became melancholy and quiet, at least it was peaceful. The boy and his sister and brother grew older and made friends and spent more time outside the family. The boy never stopped feeling sad, but slowly he built a wall against the memories and tried to stay on the other side of the wall as much as he could. Sometimes he would think of his mother, and an invisible door would open unexpectedly and he would be pulled back through it and into the gloom, but after a while, he could always go back through the door to the other side.

Then the boy met a girl and everything changed. For the first time since his mother had died, he truly believed that he might be able to stay on the good side of the wall forever. And even when the invisible door opened, as it still did now and then, he found that thanks to her, he could usually grab the doorframe and pull himself back out.

By then his brother and sister had moved on, leaving him with Alyssa and his father, whose life was drywall, and the EMS squad, and the television, and a bottle. Deep down the boy had always known that drywall and the EMS squad would be his life, too. That his father was depending on him. That he was the tape and mud that held the gypsum boards of his father's life together. That without him it would all collapse in a heap.

And the boy believed he had no choice in this matter. His deepest, greatest fear was that if Lamont Drywall and the EMS squad ended, his father would end, too. He had already experienced the loss of one parent and could not bear the thought of going through that again. Besides, now he had Callie, and as long as he had her, things would be okay.

Then high school ended and it was time for him to serve in the armed forces, just as every Lamont had since the First World War. And this, too, he had always known he would do, regardless of whether he believed in it. But he had a secret, a bad knee he'd carefully exercised to keep strong but had started to neglect, hoping that it would grow weaker and eventually get him sent home.

So he did the things he didn't want to do, went far away from home to train for a war he didn't understand and wasn't sure he believed in. And he was homesick and missed Callie horribly and counted not only the days but the hours and minutes until he could go back home and see her again.

And then, just a few weeks before he was supposed to go home, she called one night and, out of what felt like nowhere, said they were through and she didn't want to see him again. It made no sense. He felt as if he'd been blindsided. Suddenly the wall he had built collapsed and the sadness came rushing at him and enveloped him and he had nothing to grab on to. He flailed helplessly in the dark, went into shock, and became numb with disbelief. He called and wrote to Callie, but she didn't answer. It seemed unspeakably cruel and heartless for her to have broken up with him so abruptly and unexpectedly, without giving him a chance to respond.

And then, to make everything even worse, he learned that his unit would be sent overseas, to support the troops at war. He stumbled through the final weeks of Guard training like a zombie and then went home, determined to confront Callie in person, but before he could, someone else appeared in his life. Someone familiar. And she told him what he'd both suspected and feared — that while he'd been away, the girl he loved had quietly begun to see someone else.

The news was excruciating, like salt poured into a wound already too deep and painful to survive, and it produced an anger in him so extreme that he was not sure he could control it. And yet he wasn't entirely surprised. He'd seen it happen to others in his barracks. Now it was his turn.

Frightened by his own anger, and unsure that he could stand Callie's lying to him about this other guy, he decided not to confront her. Instead, he followed the example his father had set: he tried to become numb and threw himself into work, meanwhile hoping that his bad knee might prevent him from being deployed. Like his father, he might have resigned himself to nights in front of the TV, but that other girl made it clear that she had more than gossip to share with him. In fact, she had something to offer that might save his life.

chapter 48

WITH TEARS OF disbelief and confusion running down my cheeks, I stand in the motel doorway while they put Slade in the back of the patrol car and lock the doors. Then Chief Jenkins comes back toward me. "Call your mom, Callie. She's frantic."

I'm still so shocked that I can't find the words to acknowledge him. He starts toward the patrol car, then stops and turns back to me. "I'm sorry, Callie. This whole thing . . . came as a huge shock . . . to everyone involved."

"It doesn't make sense," I hear myself whimper.

He purses his lips, as if there's more he could tell me but he has decided not to. "Go home."

He gets into the patrol car. In the back, Slade stares at me with tears running down his face. He nods. I mouth the words *I love you*, and he does the same. The police cruiser rolls away.

Numb, I go back into the motel room. Slade's cell phone is lying on the night table. I open it and there on the screen is a photo of me. And it just makes me cry harder.

But finally, when I feel like I've gotten control of myself, I call Mom and tell her I'm okay and I'll be home later. She wants to know where I've been and I promise to explain that, too.

Then I sit on the unmade bed and try to make sense of it. But I can't. Slade killed Katherine? It simply can't be. The only explanation is that the police are as wrong about him as they were about me. And that means I'm still not finished. I've proved that I had nothing to do with Katherine's murder, and now I have to prove the same for Slade. But how? Where do I begin?

Lost in thought, I idly scroll through the photos on Slade's phone. They are, for the most part, photos of me. Mixed in are a few shots of young men in military uniforms, no doubt acquaintances from Guard training.

And then . . . a photo that causes me to freeze. A young woman's naked torso, shot from the chin down. A slim body with large round breasts.

It is an unmistakable glimpse of how much I still don't know.

INTERVIEW WITH DAKOTA ELIZABETH JENKINS

B—Chief of Detectives, Dennis K. Bloom
J—Dakota Elizabeth Jenkins
M—Detective Sergeant Ellis McGregor
NU—Nurse Elena Sanchez

TAPE 1, SIDE A

B   Today's date is September seventeenth and
it is now 3:43 in the afternoon. We are in
Fairchester County Hospital. Present in the
room are myself, Dennis K. Bloom, Chief of
Detectives, Soundview PD; Detective Sergeant
Ellis McGregor, Soundview PD; Dakota
Elizabeth Jenkins; and Nurse Elena
Sanchez. Would each of you please identify
yourself?

M   I'm Detective Sergeant Ellis McGregor.

J   Dakota Jenkins.

NU I am Elena Sanchez.

B   Miss Jenkins, would you please state your age
      and your social security number?

J   You want me to read the number?

B   Yes, please.

J   I am eighteen years old and my social
      security number is . . .

B   Miss Jenkins, are you prepared to acknowledge
      that you have read this form and you
      acknowledge before myself and Detective
      McGregor as witnesses that you recognize this
      form to be your Miranda warning and waiver
      statement of your rights?

J   Yes.

B   And at this time you do in fact waive your
      right to an attorney and wish to speak to
      both myself and Detective McGregor?

J   Yes.

B   Can you tell me what day this is?

J   September seventeenth.

B   And what day of the week?

J   I'm pretty sure it's Wednesday.

B   And how do you feel right now in terms of your physical condition?

J   Tired and worn out.

B   Are you of sound mind to speak to us?

J   I think so. Yes.

B   Would you please state the reason why you called us here?

J   To tell you what happened with Katherine.

M   When you say Katherine, do you mean Katherine Remington-Day?

J   Yes.

B   And when you say you want to tell us what happened, what do you mean?

J   What I think happened the night she died.

B When you say "what I think happened," is that because you're not sure?

J I'm sure of some things, but not so sure of others.

B All right.

J Where should I begin?

M Maybe with the things you're sure about.

J I'm sure that I took the knife from Katherine's house.

M What knife?

J The knife that was used to kill her. We were in the middle of a fight and I pretended I wanted to make up. But I really just wanted the knife.

B Why?

J Why did I take it?

B Yes.

J I wanted Slade to scare her.

M Would that be Slade Lamont?

J Yes.

B How would he scare her?

J He would put a stocking on his head and wear latex gloves and act like he was going to attack her.

B Where?

J In the woods behind the baseball field.

B How would he get the knife?

J I gave it to him.

B Why would he agree to take it and scare her?

J I was having sex with him. And I got my mother to help make sure he received a medical deferment so that he wouldn't be sent overseas with his National Guard unit.

M Was your mother aware of why you wanted her help?

J Oh God, no. I just told her that he was a friend of mine and that he was really scared

that the selective service board would deny
his disability claim. She said she'd look into
it. I don't even know if she actually did
more than that. He had a trick knee and might
not have been allowed to go anyway.

B   But he received the deferment?

J   Yes.

M   So you're saying that he felt he owed you a
favor?

J   Yes.

B   Why did you want to scare Katherine?

J   Because I hated her. She was an awful person
and liked to scare people and do other mean
things to them. I wanted her to have a taste
of her own medicine.

B   Why did you hate her?

J   Because I . . . I also loved her.

B   Sorry?

J   I didn't want to love her. She wanted me to
be like her and I didn't want to.

M   When you say "be like her," what do you
mean?

J   Be gay. She wanted me to be a lesbian, like
her.

B   So you wanted Slade Lamont to scare her?

J   That's what I told him I wanted him to do.
But I was really hoping he'd kill her.

B   Why?

J   Because I hoped that if he killed her, it
would all go away.

B   What would go away?

J   The feelings. I mean, about loving her. About
being a lesbian.

M   What made you think that Slade Lamont would
kill Katherine?

J   Nothing. I just hoped he would. Or at least
hurt her really badly. I knew she would
recognize him through the stocking. And
I knew Katherine would laugh at him and
taunt him, because that's the kind of
person she was.

B And you thought laughing and taunting would be enough to make him want to kill her?

J He was really depressed and angry and drinking a lot. It was all because this girl, Callie Carson, had broken up with him. But what he didn't know was that the reason she broke up with him was because Katherine had sort of forced her to do it. And I knew that given the chance, Katherine would tell him, because she loved to gloat over things like that.

M Why would Katherine force Callie Carson to break up with Slade?

J Because she had a crush on Callie. Callie was the most hetero girl ever. And she'd had the same boyfriend longer than any other girl in our grade. And Katherine felt it would be the most amazing challenge just to get Callie to try a girl. And in her mind the first step was to get her to break up with her boyfriend.

B Didn't you say before that you were having sex with Slade Lamont?

J Uh-huh.

B Why?

J Because I wanted to. I was attracted to him and there weren't that many boys I felt that way about. Plus, I told myself that as long as I was having sex with him, I couldn't be gay.

M And since Katherine had already gotten Callie to break up with him . . .

J I'd tried once before when he was with Callie, but he wouldn't do it. But as soon as I heard that Callie had broken up with him, I started to talk to him by e-mail and online, because he was still in Georgia. He kept saying that as soon as he got home from National Guard training, he was going to go see her, so finally I told him that she'd left him for another guy. That's how I got him to change his mind.

B Just to be clear, did you ever tell Slade Lamont you wanted him to kill or hurt Katherine?

J No, because I knew he'd never agree to that.

M Did Slade Lamont ever give you any impression that he wanted to do more than just scare Katherine?

J   No. He didn't even want to do that, but I
    told him that if he didn't, I would get my
    mother to rescind the deferment. Of course, I
    couldn't have really done that but he didn't
    know. He believed me.

B   So from your point of view, was anything
    about Katherine Remington-Day's death planned
    or premeditated?

J   No, nothing.

M   And as far as Slade Lamont's participation,
    do you believe anything was planned or
    premeditated?

J   Like I said, I don't think so. I think you
    can rake up a pile of dry leaves and throw
    a lit match on them and sometimes they'll
    catch fire and sometimes they won't.

M   What about Callie Carson?

B   Sorry? Oh, right. Miss Jenkins, you tried to
    put the blame for the murder on her.

J   I felt I had to shield Slade. If the
    police found out about him, he'd tell
    them about me.

M There are a few other people we'd like to ask you about.

J Okay.

M Did Mia Flom or Griffen Clemment have anything to do with your plan?

J No.

B Did they know about it?

J No.

M What about Jerry Fairman?

J I thought you already talked to him.

M We want to corroborate his story. He says he knew nothing about your plans.

J That's true. When Callie's texts came from a blocked number, I had a feeling he was involved because I'd once gotten him to help me do that.

B The texts you sent to Griffen Clemment?

J Yes. Everyone knows he can do things like that. So I called the anonymous tip line and said he might be involved.

B All right, Miss Jenkins, I just want you to
know that I really appreciate this and I just
have a few more questions. Would you please
state for the record how this interview came
to take place?

J After Katherine was killed, I knew I was at
least partly to blame, or maybe worse. I felt
like I couldn't live with myself . . . with
the idea that I was partly responsible. And
that because of me, Callie Carson might go
to jail. Yesterday it just got to be too much
for me and I took a bunch of pills. Like,
everything I could find in the medicine
cabinet. But after I took them, I realized
I'd made a mistake and I called 911. They
brought me here and pumped my stomach and
then someone came in . . . I think she said
she was the staff psychiatrist or something,
and she asked me why I'd wanted to kill
myself and it all just came out. And she
pretty much said I had to tell the police
what I'd told her.

M And since you're eighteen, you're not a minor
and don't need your parents' approval to
give this confession. But I'm curious why you
haven't consulted them.

J They were here last night and again today,

but I know what they'd want to do if I told
them the truth about what happened. They'd
want to hire a lawyer and try to get me off
without being punished. And they probably have
enough money and connections to do it, too.
But that's not what I want.

M What do you want?

J I . . . I need to take responsibility for
what I did. Otherwise I don't think I can
live with myself.

B Well, like I said, we appreciate that and
what you've told us. Now, is there anything
else you want to tell us that we haven't
asked about?

J No, I think I've told you everything.

B At any time during this interview did you
feel coerced or forced to say something you
believed was not true?

J No. I told you everything I wanted to tell
you. You didn't make me say anything I didn't
want to say. I'm just . . . really sorry
about what happened.

B Ms. Sanchez, at any time during this interview
did you observe Miss Jenkins being coerced or
forced to say anything it appeared she did
not believe was true?

NU No. It appeared to me that she gave all the
information willingly.

B It is now 4:12 on September seventeenth.
This concludes our interview with Miss Dakota
Jenkins.

chapter 50

IN THE DAYS that followed Slade's arrest, the news reported that the police had found traces of Katherine's blood on the floor mat in Slade's pickup. They'd also determined that the downward angle of the stab wounds on her body meant that Katherine's killer was likely to be taller than she was and right-handed. And probably not a short lefty, like me. Finally, they'd found evidence, Slade's DNA, under Katherine's finger-nails.

Dakota had convinced Slade to hide near the dugout with latex gloves and a stocking over his head. Before the kegger, Dakota went to Katherine's house, pretending she wanted to make up after their most recent fight. While she was there, she took one of the kitchen knives. At the kegger she met Slade by the dugout and gave him the knife. Later she told Katherine she wanted to speak to her in private about everything that had happened between them and suggested that Katherine go to the dugout and wait for her.

Katherine went to the dugout, where Slade was hiding and drinking. He heard her coming and stepped out in his disguise with the knife. But Katherine recognized him. Assuming that he was only trying to scare her, and that this was his revenge for her getting me to break up with him, she laughed and taunted him, saying that if he was stupid enough to do something like this, then she was glad she'd gotten me to break up with him, because he really didn't deserve me.

Until that moment, Slade had believed Dakota's lie—that I'd broken up with him because of another guy. But now he learned that it was Katherine who'd engineered the breakup. And he lost it. There was no other way to explain it. When he thought of all the pain she had randomly caused him, all the hope she had so easily and callously destroyed, he just plain freaked out.

There was a slight struggle, just enough for Katherine to get some traces of his skin under her nails. Then he stabbed her.

He ran across the ball field to his truck and left. Then he stopped and called Dakota to tell her what had happened and say that he was going to turn himself in to the police. But Dakota's initial reaction was that she was almost as much to blame for the murder as he was, and she convinced him not to do it. She promised him she would take care of it.

She had connections.

Dakota took care of it by sending me to the dugout to look for Katherine, then following with a crowd of kids. She took the photo of me beside Katherine's body, then posted it on the Internet.

So why were the police looking for me even though they

suspected that a tall righty had committed the murder? Because they had the bloody murder weapon with my fingerprints. Because they had the photo of me beside Katherine's body with the knife in my hand. Because I ran away from the murder scene. And because it was just possible, though unlikely, that I was ambidextrous and had knocked Katherine to the ground before stabbing her with the knife in my right hand.

Finally, there was the possibility that the killer and I had acted together. That we'd planned it, and that even though someone else had been the one who'd stabbed her, I'd been an accomplice in the crime.

chapter 51

October

THE HUGE REDBRICK Fishkill Correctional Facility sits on a hill surrounded by green lawns and double rows of tall chain-link fencing laced with razor wire. To enter you go through a metal detector and then several sets of thick doors, some made of rein-forced steel and shatterproof glass, others made from heavy steel bars.

Inside, you are in a world of sharp right angles and hard flat walls. There is no softness in prison. No comfort. Sounds echo and amplify. The click of footsteps on hard concrete, the clack of locks opening and closing, the clank of barred doors banging shut.

Inside is only the smell of body odor. There is no sweetness or perfume.

Inside, now, are my brother and Slade.

As I walk down the hall to the visiting room, I find it almost impossible to believe that this has happened. Until Sebastian attacked my father, no one in our family had ever been sent to prison. No one we knew had ever spent time in jail. We were just everyday people with everyday jobs and everyday interests. Living in an everyday town.

Here the visiting room is a series of heavy reinforced windows with partitions between them. You sit on a stool that is bolted into the floor. You pick up a phone. You look through the thick glass at the person on the other side.

For the last two years, I've come here once a week to visit Sebastian on the other side of that glass. I've grown used to that. Today, for the first time, it's Slade I'm here to see. Mr. Lamont couldn't afford his bail, so Slade will have to stay here until his trial.

When I see him through the window, my insides churn and I can't help bursting into tears. Slade's face is drawn and his jaw is covered with stubble. He presses his fingers into the corners of his eyes, as if to stem his own tears. We talk about what it's like inside. He tells me he's seen Sebastian in the cafeteria, but they haven't yet had a chance to speak. We talk about what's going on in Soundview. But the more we talk, the more I'm aware of what we're not talking about. Finally I have to bring her up.

"Dakota's parents sent her away to a private boarding school in Europe," I tell him. She's been charged with a felony—reckless endangerment—but unlike Slade's dad, her parents were able to afford the bail that guarantees she'll return for her trial.

When I tell Slade about Dakota's going away, he nods and stares down at the counter on his side of the window.

"Slade?"

He looks up, his eyes sad, his face etched with regret.

"That story you told me, about how Dakota hit on one of the workers doing construction in her kitchen?"

He nods. "It was me."

"And you didn't tell me because she was supposed to be my friend? Or at least we were in the same crowd?"

Again he nods. "It was back when you were still happy about being with them."

"And then, when you came back from Guard training . . ." There's no reason to state the obvious—that Dakota was waiting to tell him that I was seeing someone else, but that she was there for him, and that her mother could help him get a deferment so he wouldn't be deployed. Slade stares down at the counter again and I can only blame myself. I'd broken his heart and he'd come home feeling hopeless and in agony, and there was Dakota, sending him naked photos of herself, offering her version of comfort.

"You stopped doing your knee exercises when you found out your unit was going to be deployed?" I ask.

He shakes his head. "I stopped way before that. Like, from the moment I told Dad I'd go into the Guard. First I was hoping I'd fail the entrance physical. I mean, if I did, Dad couldn't blame me, right? But the doctors okayed me. Then I hoped the knee would blow out during training. I could feel it getting weaker, but it didn't give. And then, when they told us we were being deployed, I really freaked."

"And that's when Dakota said her mother could help you get the deferment from the medical review board?"

"Yeah."

The next part is difficult for me to put into words: "After the kegger, why didn't you turn yourself in right away?"

He looks away. "I felt like . . . like it was all everyone else's fault. Like it was Katherine's fault for making you break up with me. And it was Dakota's fault for lying about you having another boyfriend. And it was your fault, Cal, for doing what Katherine wanted you to do. Because that's what started it all in the first place. Like you and them and everyone else were the reason I lost control with Katherine. Like you and them were to blame for everything that happened. And then I thought about my dad and what it would do to him. I mean, me being arrested for murder. I knew it would kill him. And then, instead of having one death on my head, I'd have two."

"And then you found out what Dakota meant by taking care of it?"

"Yeah, by putting the blame on you. And then you called and told me you still loved me and it was like . . . like I realized we were in it together. Like, how could I blame you for what Katherine got you to do when I thought about what Dakota had gotten me to do? You know? It was like we'd both been totally manipulated. Completely outclassed. Like we were two little kids making sand castles with plastic toys and along came Katherine and Dakota with a backhoe and a bulldozer. We never stood a chance."

"And then you helped me because you didn't want me to be blamed for killing Katherine any more than you wanted to take the blame yourself?" I ask.

His head bobs up and down as he practically radiates regret.

"But you had to know that by doing that, you'd also be forcing the police to look for someone else, and that you'd be one of the suspects," I tell him.

He shakes his head. "I thought you'd go for the self-defense thing. And that would have been the end of it right there. Case closed. And then, when you said you wouldn't agree to that, I was hoping that maybe it would be neither of us. The cops would figure out that you couldn't have done it and they wouldn't know where else to look. I mean, the only other person who knew what really happened was Dakota, and I was certain she'd be the last one to tell."

"Guess she surprised us both," I say.

He nods. "I knew something was up when they impounded my truck and asked me to come down to the station for finger-prints and a DNA test. And that's when I grabbed a bunch of clothes, got some money, and took the train to Montauk."

He looks up, his eyes red-rimmed and watery. "I know what you're thinking, Cal. I left you. You're the only one I've ever loved and I still took off. But I wasn't going to stay away that long. I knew I'd eventually come back and turn myself in. There's no way I could have lived with myself knowing what I did. I just"—a strange, sad, ironic smile appears on his lips—"I just . . . wanted to spend some time as a commercial fisherman first."

My eyes are also filled with tears. "We both made mistakes, Slade. Big ones."

On the other side of the window, he wipes the tears from his eyes. "Can you forgive me?"

"Can *you* forgive *me*?" I ask.

"Yeah." He places his hand against the glass.

I press my hand against the other side. "I love you, Slade."

"I love you, Shrimp."

Our visit ends. Slade is taken back to his cell, and I leave the facility. It is a bright, clear October day and the sky is blue. In the distance the hillsides are covered with green and here and there a splotch of yellow or red, the first signs of fall. Once I was afraid I wouldn't be able to wait for Slade for twelve months. Now I may have to wait for years. But I feel like I can. I have seen and experienced more terrible things in the first seventeen years of my life than most people see and experience in a lifetime. If there is anyone who has the right to give up or take the easy way out, it is me. And yet I persist. I will do whatever has to be done. I will wait as long as I must.

If you enjoyed *Blood on My Hands,*

take a look at an excerpt from

Todd Strasser's latest thriller, *Kill You Last*

By the author of *Wish You Were Dead*

TODD STRASSER

kill you last

A TEXT SHOWED up . . . from Gabriel: **Thx 4 inviting me 2 the party. W2 meet again? 121?**

That caught me by surprise. I could only assume that the quick kiss I'd given him after the party had smoothed out the earlier rough spots. It was flattering to think that he still liked me, but then I thought about the warnings both Whit and Roman had given me about him. I was thinking about how to answer him when an e-mail popped up from vengeance13772388@gmail.com: **I like you, Shelby Sloan. If I have to kill you, I'll kill you last.**

I almost cried out. My hands gripped the edge of the desk chair and my heart thudded heavily in my chest as I stared at the ominous words, rereading them over and over.

Someone was threatening to kill me.

"IT'S THE THIRD time this year a girl has gone missing after saying she was going to a mall to meet someone," my friend Roman whispered. "Tell me that's not weird."

"That's not weird," I said. We were sitting at a table in the library, killing time, waiting for school to end. Roman was on her iPad, engaging in her favorite pastime—researching crimes against young women.

"I don't think anyone's noticed," Roman went on as if I hadn't even spoken. "Because the girls are all from different cities."

I felt my BlackBerry vibrate and slid it into my lap to read the screen. It was an e-mail, which was strange, since none of my friends ever e-mailed anymore. Stranger still because it was from someone calling themself vengeance13772388@gmail.com. *This is weird*, I thought.

"Shelby, are you even listening to me?" Roman got huffy.

"Just hold on a second," I said, then opened the e-mail:

**Ur a sweet, nice girl with ur perfect house
and riding in daddys ferrari. 2 bad u
dont no what he really does.**

Roman hooked her black hair behind her ear and looked at me curiously. She must have seen the perplexed expression on my face. "What is it?"

I handed the BlackBerry to her under the table.

"Creep show," she said, handing it back. "Who sends e-mails? And what does he mean by what your dad really does?"

"How do you know it's a *he*?" I asked.

"The sweet, nice-girl part. A girl wouldn't write that." Roman was my best friend and really smart, but sometimes the stuff that came out of her mouth was off-the-charts bizarre.

"Why not?"

"She just wouldn't."

"That makes no sense."

"Says you," Roman replied with a dismissive shrug. "Anyway, I bet I'm the only one who's put together this thing with the three missing girls."

"Just like you were the only one who figured out that the shark that bit off that girl's arm in Hawaii was the same one who killed a girl two years earlier in Australia because both girls were blonde?"

"I never said that," Roman insisted. "I just said, wouldn't it be interesting if that was the case?"

I rolled my eyes doubtfully. "The shark that preferred blondes."

"Maybe it thought it was doing the world a favor," quipped Roman. "But seriously, this is completely different. These girls are all from the northeast—Hartford, Connecticut, Scranton, Pennsylvania, and Trenton, New Jersey. And they all left school at lunch to meet someone at a mall."

"Uh, hello?" I pointed at the e-mail on my Blackberry. "Have we already forgotten that I just got a very weird e-mail?"

"Write back," Roman said.

"And say what? Who are you and why did you write this? If he wanted me to know who he was he wouldn't have used this creepy vengeance at Gmail address."

"Say that you already know what your dad does and you're dealing with it, thank you very much."

"Good idea. Thanks." I thumbed in the message.

Roman rested her elbows on the table and plunked her chin in her hands, looking bored. "It's probably just a joke."

"Maybe." I pressed send.

Suddenly Roman lifted her head. "Guess who just came in?"

I turned my head. Chris Clarke, tall, broad-shouldered, and husky, all-state tight end with a 3.9 GPA, was looking at the magazine rack. When he saw me, he smiled and waved. I did the same.

"He's interested," Roman whispered.

"I know." Chris and I had been exchanging looks and smiles for the past week.

"You'd be such a perfect couple," Roman whispered again. "Has he said anything?"

"Not yet," I said. "So far it's been all smiles and nods."

"Maybe he's waiting for you to make the first move," Roman said.

3

Before I could respond, my phone vibrated for the second time. It was another message from him. I quickly opened it and found one word: **Liar**.

AFTER SCHOOL I drove to Dad's studio and parked next to his bright red Ferrari. That car, I sometimes joked, was my only serious competition for his affections. I'd just gotten out of my Jeep when two men I'd never seen before came out of the studio's back door. They got into a dark green sedan, with a laptop mounted inside, and drove away. It didn't take a rocket surgeon to figure out that they were detectives.

I let myself in and started down the wood-paneled hallway lined with autographed headshots of famous models and actors. Almost all the photos were autographed to Dad in black Sharpie with personal thanks and salutations. In the kitchenette, Mercedes was making coffee. Petite and pretty, with dark hair and gold hoop earrings, she was Dad's resident stylist and general office gofer.

"Hola, Mercedes." I stopped in the doorway. "¿Cómo se Angelo?"

Angelo was her little boy and, at the mention of his name, Mercedes would usually react with a big smile and a story about his latest achievement or mischievous behavior. But today her brown eyes slid away and she fingered the gold cross on her neck. "Está bien, gracias." Her English was fairly good, but I liked to practice my Spanish with her. After high school I planned to travel around Central America for a few months before starting college.

I wondered if Mercedes' lack of enthusiasm had something to do with those detectives. "What did they want?" I asked.

"You should ask your father."

Her solemn mood was unsettling. "Okay," I said. "How do you say, give Angelo a hug for me?"

Mercedes smiled weakly. "Angelo dar un abrazo para mí. Gracias, Miss Shelby."

I continued down the hall to the office where Janet, Dad's modeling agent and office manager, was standing at a file cabinet with her back to me. I didn't want to startle her so I knocked gently on the door frame.

Despite my cautious approach Janet jumped, the stack of files in her arms spilling to the floor, papers and headshots going everywhere. "Ahhh!" she gasped.

"Sorry," I said.

Someone else might have said, "It's not your fault." But Janet stared haplessly at the papers, photos, and files on the floor. Gray roots showed along the part in her brown hair. "Now what am I going to do? How am I ever going to figure out what goes back in which file?"

"I'll help." I kneeled down to gather up the files.

"No!" she practically barked. "Leave it alone."

"But—"

6

"I said, leave it, *please*, Shelby?"

You could see that she was in an extra fragile mood today. When I straightened up I saw that she was trembling. I knew the tiniest things could sometimes send her into histrionics, but it usually took more than a few dropped files.

"What a freaking day," she groaned, and plopped down on the corner of her desk, crossing her arms tightly and looking jittery. Like the floor, the desk was covered with disorganized papers and photos. You had to wonder why Dad hired someone so disorganized to be his office manager.

"What's going on?" I asked.

"Two girls are missing. The Dicks wanted to know what we knew about them."

"Were they models?" I asked, wondering if the girls Janet referred to could possibly be related to the missing girls Roman had spoken of at school. If that was the case, Roman would have a field day.

"We did their headshots," Janet said.

"What happened to them?"

She gestured with a shaky hand to a file of photos and papers on the floor. "They're probably there somewhere."

"Not the headshots," I said. "I meant, what happened to the girls?"

"Who knows?"

Across the hall, the door to the photo studio opened and Gabriel Gressen, ridiculously gorgeous hunk, part-time model, and Dad's photo assistant, came out with a plate of Chinese food. I felt my heart flutter . . . and not because I found beef with broccoli irresistible.

7

WITH HIS DARK eyes, wavy black hair, and chiseled looks, Gabriel Gressen was nothing short of drop-dead dreamy. Half the reason I stopped by Dad's studio so often was to gaze upon his statuesque beauty.

Gabriel crossed the hall and stepped into the office, holding out the food. "Anyone interested?"

If only he'd been offering himself, I thought.

"I'll take it." Janet reached for the plate and began to eat hungrily with her fingers.

Gabriel glanced at the papers on the floor as if it was nothing unusual, then smiled at me. "Hey."

My insides turning to Jell-O, I calmly replied, "Hi, what's up?"

"Big glamour shoot today."

"Really? Who?"

"General Tso and his friends Moo shu and Ginger."

"Hardy har har." I showed him I got the joke, then pointed across the hall at the photo studio door. "Can I go in?"

"Sure. I don't think the prawns'll mind if you see them un-dressed."

I went into the photo studio, which, not surprisingly, smelled like a Chinese restaurant. Dad was focusing a camera on a bright-ly lit plate of chow mien. On a table nearby were a dozen other Asian dishes waiting their turn in the spotlight.

"This for a food magazine?" I asked.

"Not exactly." Dad fired a few shots. Strobes popped and flashed, leaving spots in my eyes.

"Advertising?"

"Sort of." He repositioned the plate. "A menu. For the Whacky Wok."

The Whacky Wok was a hole-in-the-wall take-out place on a side street in Soundview. A big sign over the counter displayed photos of the various menu items along with their correspond-ing numbers. A wisp of sadness crept over me. In the world of commercial photography, shooting menus was about as low as you could go, especially for a man who'd once done $10,000-a-day fashion shoots. More pops and flashes followed, then Dad replaced the chow mien with what looked like cashew chicken.

"What's with the detectives and the missing girls?" I asked.

"You got me." He adjusted a light. "Seems that we did some shots for their books."

"Books" was model-business slang for the portfolios in which models carried their photos.

"Did they say what they think happened to them?"

"Nah, just asked us some questions." Again strobes popped and flashed. I thought of mentioning the missing girls Roman had mentioned earlier at school, but it was obvious that Dad didn't think it was a big deal. Besides, there was something else on my mind—that strange e-mail.

"Interesting," Dad said after I showed it to him on my Black-Berry.

"Any idea what it means?"

He rubbed his hands together, made his eyes bulge, and grinned maniacally. "I could tell you, my dear, but then I'd have to kill you."

"I'm serious, Dad."

"Seriously? Not a clue. Probably just someone playing with your head." He picked up his camera. "Gotta get this done before the food starts to look soggy. Feel free to take anything I've finished shooting home."

"You won't be home for dinner?"

"Looks like I'll be here pretty late."

I accepted the news with resignation. Dad always had a reason to stay away from home. And it wasn't just late nights at the studio, but weekends, too, when he'd go out of town to shoot weddings and anniversaries.

I put my arms around his neck and hugged him. "Why don't you have dinner with us tonight?"

"I still have a lot to do here," he said, hugging me back. "But I promise that Sunday we'll do something special, okay? Just the two of us?"

I kissed him on the cheek, took some Chinese food, and went back out to the hall. There was no sign of Gabriel. In the office Janet was thumbing through a file cabinet, the contents of the dropped files still scattered all over the floor, and the half-finished plate of beef with broccoli on her desk. I thought of saying good-bye, but didn't want to risk startling her again.

As I passed the kitchenette, Gabriel stepped out. I practically wound up in his arms. "Ah!" I laughed nervously and backed away, feeling my face grow hot. "Sorry!"

He smiled calmly, as if women stepped into his arms on a daily occurrence, which, come to think of it, was probably true. "Nothing to be sorry about. That was nice." His words had a slightly teasing quality. Meanwhile, those dark eyes burrowed in. "You look pretty."

"Thanks," I said, and almost replied, "you look gorgeous."

"Got a boyfriend?" he asked.

"No one special."

"That's surprising."

"Not if you saw what Soundview High has to offer." That wasn't really the case, but I never let the truth get in the way of snappy repartee.

He smiled again. This wasn't the first time I'd felt attraction vibes emanating from him. But something always seemed to hold him back. I suspected it was because he worked for Dad and was worried that if we started dating and things went sour it might make for an awkward situation.

Which was too bad.

Maybe I'd have to talk Dad into firing him.

Just kidding.

Wicked Wings

A LIZZIE GRACE NOVEL

ISBN: **978-0-6484973-0-1**

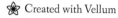 Created with Vellum

With thanks to:

The Lulus
Indigo Chick Designs
Hot Tree Editing
Debbie from DP+
Robyn E.
Julianne P.
Marjorie A.
The lovely ladies from Central Vic Writers
Lori from Cover Reveal Designs for the lovely cover